Pretty Maids All in a Row

When Jessica Randal, a West End actress, accompanied her biographer husband to the country for a month's research, she fully expected to be bored, especially since her leg was in plaster following an accident on their honeymoon. Yet within a week of their arrival she'd learned they were renting the house of a murder victim, and that there was an unknown rapist at large, who was obsessed with nursery rhymes.

The different levels of the village, both geographical and social, seemed equally at risk: Carrie Speight the cleaner and her hairdresser sister Della; the Matron and staff of the Old People's Home; the wealthy Markham family; and, increasingly, Jessica herself, apparently singled out by the rapist.

Since she might have met the man socially, Jessica regarded all her neighbours with growing suspicion. Still worse, there'd been no trouble in the village before they came, and she began to wonder, as others already did, how well she knew her new husband.

Once again, Chief Inspector Webb and Sergeant Jackson pit their wits against a cunning adversary. By the time they unmask him, the innocent world of nursery rhymes has, for the village of Westridge, been contaminated for ever.

ANTHEA FRASER

Pretty Maids All in a Row

COLLINS, 8 GRAFTON STREET, LONDON W1

William Collins Sons & Co. Ltd
London · Glasgow · Sydney · Auckland
Toronto · Johannesburg

First published 1986
© Anthea Fraser 1986

British Library Cataloguing in Publication Data

Fraser, Anthea
    Pretty maids all in a row.—(Crime Club)
    I. Title
    823′.914[F]   PR6056.R28/

ISBN 0 00 231443 6

Photoset in Linotron Baskerville by
Rowland Phototypesetting Ltd
Bury St Edmunds, Suffolk
Printed in Great Britain by
William Collins Sons & Co. Ltd, Glasgow

CHAPTER 1

His teeth were chattering, though it was unbearably hot in the room and he was bathed in sweat. Pulses throbbed sickeningly throughout his body as panic engulfed him, closing his throat, pricking his scalp, furring the inside of his mouth. It took a conscious effort of will to remain where he was, and not go running naked out of the house.

She had drawn the curtains, and through their thin material the September sun blazed undiminished, filling the room with a rosy glow. He'd laughed at her for drawing them, since they were on the first floor. 'Expecting the window-cleaner?' he'd asked her. Now, he was grateful for the thin screen they offered.

He stood in the middle of the room, drawing deep breaths and being careful not to look at the bed. That was better. His brain was beginning to function again. There was no hurry. Important to remember that. No one was likely to come to the house, and he wasn't expected anywhere. Plenty of time to work things out.

Still with his back to the bed, he went to the chair and, feeling in his jacket pocket, drew out cigarettes and matches. No one had seen him arrive, he was sure. He moved to the window and put his eye to the small gap between the curtains. Across the narrow lane a patch of uncultivated land rose towards the road on the next level, but to right and left small cottages basked, humped under their thatches, in the hot sunshine. It wouldn't be safe to move till dark, which was—what?—a good four or five hours yet. Plenty of time to plan, to avoid mistakes.

Testing himself, he turned back to the bed. She lay as he had left her, sweat still glistening on her body, the lurid pink glow unkindly highlighting sinews on her neck and grey at the roots of her hair. She'd been a good lay, though, he thought dispassionately. Plenty of experience. A pity, but he'd had no alternative. Impossible to rely on her keeping quiet, and he'd too much to lose if she talked.

He tipped a lozenge of ash into a little china dish on the dressing-table. Remember to rinse that later. Through the mirror was a looking-glass room, the reverse of normality. Appropriate, really, in the circumstances. He could see the bed with the figure on it, and, centre stage, his own bare body, cigarette in hand.

He'd feel better after a shower. Easier to think clearly with his clothes on.

Slowly the hours passed. Quite early on he had drawn back the curtains, standing to one side as he did so. It would not be possible, later, to switch on lights, so everything must be completed in daylight, and he had to make it seem she'd gone on holiday. Now, as at last blueness filtered through the air, he had only to wait for it to thicken, and he could go.

Methodically he reviewed his actions. A suitcase, removed from the top of the wardrobe, had been packed with clothes and toiletries and stood ready by the front door, a mackintosh draped over it. On top of the mackintosh lay a neatly typed and stamped envelope. He'd post that once he'd got rid of the body. Upstairs, bed linen and towels had been changed and the soiled items bundled into a black plastic bag he'd found under the sink. The contents of a second bag were more gruesome but, after dressing the body, he'd managed to bundle her in. She was sitting with her knees up and torso bowed over. There was a surprising amount of room.

He'd also emptied and rinsed the milk bottle and cleaned out the fridge. The dahlias on the hearth, just beginning to droop, had been ruthlessly tipped into the bin and the vase washed. Windows were secured throughout the house, which he'd gone round in rubber gloves from the kitchen, wiping all the surfaces he'd touched.

'Upstairs and downstairs and in my lady's chamber!' That gave him an idea and he laughed aloud in the still house. Returning to the typewriter, he inserted a fresh sheet of paper and punched out a few lines. Not easy in rubber gloves, but he managed it. He read through what he had written, smiling to himself:

Here comes a candle to light you to bed,
And here comes a chopper to chop—off—your—head.

He ripped it out of the machine and, fumbling open the black bag, stuffed it into the pocket of her dress. Wonder what they'd make of that, if and when she was found.

Her car still stood in the drive, the keys on the kitchen table where she'd dropped them. Useful, that. Restlessly he checked the house again. The stage was set. The bedroom, with its crisp sheets and neat counterpane, looked innocent of all violence, all terror, pain and fear. There was nothing anywhere to arouse suspicion.

Nodding with satisfaction, he went downstairs for the last time and, holding his breath, opened the front door. It was raining, a hissing torrent of silver needles glinting in the light from the street lamp. Swearing, he lifted the mackintosh from the suitcase and, shaking it out, draped it hood-like over his head and shoulders. He was ready to go.

Carrie lay on her back in the darkness, listening to the rain sluicing and drumming outside. She imagined the familiar garden, alien by night, with rivulets coursing along the paths, and trees bowed down by the torrent. She hadn't put the deckchair away, either. Its seat would be a miniature pool, the ancient canvas, faded with the suns of uncounted summers, sagging under the weight of water.

Her imagination moved from the confines of the garden to the village beyond its walls. The waterfall near The Orange Tree must be a foaming Niagara by now and the roads snaking zig-zag fashion down the hillside, treacherous streams of water. She hoped Mrs Cowley was having better weather, wherever she was.

Carrie frowned in the darkness, her tongue exploring the throbbing tooth whose pain had woken her. It was odd, her going off like that without telling anyone. She hadn't mentioned it on Tuesday—or perhaps she had. Carrie'd been in no state to remember much, after her visit to the dentist. And Mrs Cowley'd been so kind, running her home in the car and even coming in with her, to make sure she had aspirins. If she *had* mentioned going away, Carrie accepted that she wouldn't have registered it.

It was no good, she'd have to go down for some more pills. Softly, in her bare feet, she padded down the stairs and through the kitchen to the bathroom extension beyond. Her face in the mirror over the basin was gaunt and pale, eyes dark-circled with pain. She shook two tablets into her palm, bent her mouth to the tap and drank the tepid water, shuddering. One thing, at least she could sleep in. Tomorrow was her day for Hinckley's, but with Mrs Cowley away she could indulge herself.

Cautiously, standing on the cold linoleum, Carrie prodded her tooth again. Its deep-seated throbbing shot pain up the side of her jaw and behind her ear. She liked going to Hinckley's, though. Mrs Cowley had such pretty things, it was a pleasure to dust them.

No one in the village remembered who 'Hinckley' had been. Possibly the builder or original owner of the cottage, which had stood in its patch of garden for nearly two hundred years. But Westridge didn't believe in change, and no matter who the present owner, Hinckley's retained its name. In the same way, the post office was known as Miller's, though Fred Miller had been in his grave ten years.

She sighed, snapped off the light and made her way back through the dark kitchen and up the stairs, wincing as the top one creaked beneath her weight.

'Carrie?'

'It's all right—I went down for some aspirins.'

She snuggled back into bed, drawing the sheet up to her chin. The psychological effect of the pills was swifter than their therapeutic value and already she was drifting into sleep. Her last waking thought was that perhaps there'd be a postcard from Mrs Cowley in a day or so, letting them know when to expect her back.

Jessica Selby leant her head against the back of the seat and closed her eyes. The two-hour drive from London had tired her more than she'd admitted and her leg, encased in plaster and laid along the back seat, ached intolerably.

Matthew's voice roused her. 'All right, darling?'

She smiled at him in the mirror. 'I shall be.'

'Not bumped about too much? It's rougher going, now we're off the motorway.'

'I'm fine,' she lied. What a way to end a honeymoon, swathed in bandages in a Swiss hospital!

'Poor love, this couldn't be worse timing, could it? You should be recuperating in comfort at home, instead of being whisked to the back of beyond like this. But the deadline can't be extended, and I'm selfish enough to want you with me.'

'So I should think. We've hardly had time to get to know each other yet!'

Matthew laughed as she'd intended, but she realized with a jolt that she'd spoken the truth. Eight weeks ago, they'd not even met. They didn't actually know each other at all. Admittedly they knew about each other, but that was hardly the same. She was aware, for instance, that Matthew was a successful biographer, with several bestsellers to his name; that he'd previously been married for fourteen years and divorced for two, and had a son and daughter, whose existence she preferred to ignore. And for his part he knew her to be an actress, also with a broken marriage behind her, though thankfully no children. It was a shaky enough basis on which to bind themselves to each other.

Her eyes returned to his reflected face, unsmiling now as

he concentrated on his driving. But perhaps because of her tiredness, the focus of her gaze shifted, and for the fraction of a second she seemed to be looking at a stranger. Then his eyes met hers again and he smiled, dissolving her incipient panic, and she silently scolded herself. Over-dramatizing, as usual. Keep your histrionics for the stage, my girl, they're too wearing to live with!

'Is it a pretty village, this Westridge?' she asked.

'I was more struck by its convenience, with the Hall only ten minutes away. But yes, I suppose it's pretty. It's built on several levels, running along the ridge of a hill. From the top road, you look down on the houses and gardens below, and beyond them to the farms on the floor of the valley. But when I say it's convenient, I'm speaking personally. It won't be for you, my love, though since you're not mobile anyway, it shouldn't make much difference. And the cottage has a garden, so at least you can relax and learn your lines in peace.'

Jessica was silent. A Londoner born and bred, she suspected that a month in the country would bore her to distraction, even with two good legs to get about on. The idea of being stuck in a cottage garden day after day didn't appeal at all. Still, if Matthew had to be up here for his research, she'd no option but to come too and make the best of it.

'I hope the house is suitable,' she said after a moment.

'It sounds perfect. It has the requisite cloakroom downstairs, so you need only go up and down stairs once a day, and there's a room which I can use as a study.'

'Lucky it should come on the market just as we needed it.'

'Fate!' he said with a laugh. 'I realized when I was up last week that the village would be perfect for us, but the agents had nothing on their books. Which is why I snapped this up as soon as they phoned, without even seeing it.'

'And the agent's meeting us at the pub, you said?'

'That's right. We'll have to go through the inventory.'

They turned off the main road and Jessica, reading the signpost, leant forward.

'We've a fair way to go yet,' Matthew warned her.

The road on which they found themselves was narrow and winding, with passing places. For a while there were no buildings on their right, and they had an uninterrupted view across the valley to the multicoloured woods on the opposite slopes. On their left, cottages were built against the hillside, the base of their garden walls at shoulder height. By craning her head, Jessica could see steep paths leading up to porched doorways, many of them overhung with flaming curtains of Virginia creeper. Flowers of all colours abounded, both in the gardens and along the verges of the road.

The descent became steeper, with houses on their right now, larger and more modern than the earlier cottages. At intervals short, steep roads led down to the next level, but Matthew followed the one they were on until it forked at the end of its descent. The left-hand turning, he informed her, led through woods to Sandon Hall.

'And,' he added, following the right-hand curve, 'here we are at last.'

He turned off the road beside a handsome old building and followed the arrow to the inn car park. A large sign, depicting a stylized tree dotted with red blobs, announced it to be The Orange Tree.

'Just in time for lunch,' Matthew commented with satisfaction.

The young man who was waiting for them was stocky and red-haired, with bright hazel eyes. He came forward with his hand out.

'Mr and Mrs Selby? Julian Bayliss, J. R. Bayliss and Son.'

'Are you pressed for time, Mr Bayliss? If not, I suggest we have lunch before going to the house. As you see, my wife is convalescing and the drive has been a strain for her.' He turned to Jessica. 'And I'd further suggest, darling, that when we've eaten, you relax here with coffee while we get the inventory business out of the way. You're in need of a rest, I'm sure.'

She was more than happy to comply. The thought of going through an entire house, however small, item by item, exhausted her.

After lunch, therefore, Matthew procured for her the privacy of the inn parlour and, relaxing luxuriously on the comfortable old sofa, she surprised herself by falling soundly asleep.

It was after three when he returned alone. 'All set, sweetheart. Hinckley Cottage is ours for the next four weeks. Let's go and take possession.'

As they turned right out of the driveway, Jessica saw they were driving back the way they had come, but along the lower road. The houses they'd passed that morning rose above them against the skyline. Then Matthew turned into a narrow driveway and switched off the engine. Silence rushed in on her, not the fleeting absence of sound you might experience in London, but the deep, rushing silence of the country, penetrating mind and body, and seeming even to silence one's heartbeat. Matthew swivelled in his seat and smiled at her.

'Welcome home, my sweet!' he said.

Ten minutes later, after a brief inspection of the ground floor, she had been settled on another sofa, this time in the main room into which the front door opened directly. Two other rooms led off it, one a blessedly up-to-date kitchen with the promised cloakroom in its back porch, and the other a dining-room-cum-study, which Matthew proposed to take over.

'Look, there's even a typewriter!' he'd said. 'If I'd known that, I shouldn't have had to hump my own beast from home.'

The living-room itself was prettily decorated in keeping with its age, even if there was, for Jessica's taste, an over-preponderance of pink. Lovely old wood gleamed richly in the afternoon sun, and the ancient fireplace was screened by an ornamental vase. She could fill it with flowers from the garden. On either side of the chimney-breast were shelved alcoves, and from where she sat, some of the ornaments displayed appeared to be Meissen. A trusting owner, to leave them to their fate with unknown tenants.

Her eyes came to rest on the steep flight of stairs in the corner of the room. Certainly she'd be incapable of tackling those alone. When Matthew was out, she'd be confined to the ground floor.

'Now,' he said, coming in with the cases and dumping them at the foot of the stairs, 'having been instructed in the workings of the cooker, I shall make you a cup of tea.'

She made to rise, but he stopped her.

'But darling, that at least is something I can do!'

'Not today, and probably not for the rest of the week. Doctor's orders, remember: "Thou shalt not wash dishes, nor yet feed the swine." We'll find someone in the village to cook and clean for us.'

He disappeared into the kitchen, whistling as he filled the kettle and set out cups and saucers. Jessica watched him as he came back and positioned a low table within her reach, trying to see him dispassionately, rather than with the eyes of love. He was, after all, just a man—-slightly above average height, with a lean build and fair hair already receding. Self-mockingly, she pursued her inventory: wide bony forehead, slightly lined; prominent cheekbones; intelligent, impatient eyes. Why, in the name of all that was wonderful, was he so important to her? She only knew he was.

She said softly, 'Matthew Selby, I love you very much.'

He bent to kiss her. 'And I you. Never forget that.' He straightened and patted his pockets. "Damn, I'm out of cigarettes. When we've had tea I'll go and get some, and order a daily paper at the same time. We mustn't lose touch with the outside world.'

*

Kathy Markham paused, wooden spoon in hand, as she heard the front door close. 'That you, darling?'

'Who else are you expecting?' Her husband came into the kitchen, and she lifted her face for his kiss.

'It could have been William. He went fishing with the Rowe twins, but he should be back by now.'

'I saw him coming up Green Lane as I passed. He won't be long.'

'You might have given him a lift.'

'In that condition? Not on your life. I'd advise you to make him strip on the back step.' Guy stood at the kitchen window, staring down his sloping garden to the lower road and the cottages that crouched there. 'Had a good day?'

'So-so. Angie's a bit fraught about that French she was set, but it's her own fault. She shouldn't have left it till the last minute, as I've been telling her the whole holiday.'

'Baudelaire, isn't it? Pretty heavy going.'

'That's hardly the point.' Kathy sampled the casserole and shook in some more salt. 'By the way, there's a new man in the village. He came into Miller's while I was buying stamps. From what I heard, he and his wife will be at Hinckley's for the next month or so.'

'I didn't know Freda took in lodgers. At least, not with their wives!'

'But Freda's not there. Apparently she's gone off somewhere, and left instructions for the place to be let.'

'Bit sudden, wasn't it? She never mentioned it when we saw her last week.'

'Well, you know Freda. She's probably got herself a new man and gone waltzing off with him. I do wish she'd pull herself together. It's two years now since Bruce left her. She can't go on like this indefinitely.'

'Who says she can't? Several devoted husbands round here avail themselves of her services.'

Kathy stared at him. 'You *are* joking, aren't you?'

'Indeed I'm not.'

'But that's awful! Who are they?'

'Ah, that'd be telling! Anyway, it's only hearsay, and highly slanderous.'

'For heaven's sake, Guy! Now you've gone that far, you might as well finish it.'

'All I'm saying is, she could run quite a lucrative line in blackmail, if she'd a mind to.'

'But you—' She broke off as a small figure materialized beyond the frosted glass of the back door. 'See to William, will you, darling? Make sure he takes his boots off before he comes in—Carrie washed this floor today.'

And as the concerns of her family took precedence, Freda Cowley and her affairs were pushed temporarily from Kathy's mind.

At The Willows Residential Home on the top road, old Mrs Southern was being difficult again.

'She wouldn't touch her supper,' Nurse Ironside reported to Cook, exasperation in her voice. 'And she's still got this bee in her bonnet about it being Christmas.'

Cook clucked disapprovingly and tipped the contents of the plate into the slops bucket. 'Waste of good food, that is. I don't make my cheese pies for Carrie Speight's hens. Christmas, indeed! If she thinks I'm cooking turkey at the beginning of September, she can think again. What started her on that, anyway?'

'Who ever knows what starts Mrs Southern off?' The nurse paused, ashamed of her outburst. 'Oh, she's a nice enough old thing, plummy voice and all, but as stubborn as they're made. Once she's got something into her head, there's no way of shifting it. But when I asked why she thought it was Christmas, that cunning look came over her face and she wouldn't tell me. Just kept saying, "Aren't there any presents for me? I've not even had a card this year." She was quite upset about it.'

Cook tutted resignedly. 'Going round the twist, if you ask me. We'll have her as daft as Miss Sampson, you mark my words.'

Pammy Ironside shook her head. 'No, you're wrong there. She gets some odd ideas now and then but she's bright enough. Reads everything we give her, and without glasses, too, for all she's well past eighty. Eyes like a hawk.' Pammy giggled. 'She caused quite an upset with Ivy yesterday, insisting there was dust on the dresser. She was right, too —there was! It's tragic, really, her being paralysed like that. Like being a prisoner inside her own body.'

'Give over—you make my hair stand on end, the way you talk!' Cook hesitated, then said gruffly, 'Think she'd get some bread and milk down, if I did some for her?'

Pammy smiled. 'I think she just might. Bless you, Cook.'

In his little cottage opposite the post office, Police Constable Ted Frost, comfortably paunched and looking forward to retirement, locked up for the night. It had been a good day. The boy had brought some corn cobs back from the farm, a present from Mr Davis, and Margie had cooked them just right. He was partial to corn on the cob, even though he couldn't regard it as English. Still, with salt and pepper, and plenty of butter dripping over it, it took some beating, that he would admit. And tonight it was followed by rabbit, which Benjie'd shot himself.

A lot to be said for being based in the country, Ted reflected complacently. All very well for the Smart Alecs in Shillingham and Broadminster, zooming round in their Pandas. He was quite happy with Westridge and his old bike, thanks all the same.

'Go on, Jack, I'm surprised you don't die of boredom!' they teased him, at intermittent training sessions. (He'd been 'Jack' to his colleagues, for obvious reasons, since the day he joined the Force.) Well, it was all right for them to spend their lives chasing bank robbers and the like, but he was too old for that now, and truth to tell had never really fancied it. The village bobby, everyone's friend. That was more his line. Apart from the odd complaints of 'scrumping',

Westridge was a law-abiding place, and he'd nothing to complain of in that.

The old black retriever thumped his tail as his master checked the back door. When Margie wasn't looking, a portion of rabbit had found its way into his bowl. Ted winked conspiratorially at the animal. Wonder if old Rover associated the tasty morsel with those leaping, flashing forms he'd chased so enthusiastically in his younger days? But that was being fanciful. Of course he didn't.

Chuckling to himself, the policeman started up the stairs, pausing as he always did at the window on the half-landing, from which vantage-point he could see half the village spread before him. Even as he watched, several of the lights went out, one after another. Well, it was almost eleven, and folks were up early hereabouts.

Belching comfortably, he went on his way to bed.

CHAPTER 2

Jessica stood in her dressing-gown at the bedroom window. Immediately below was the cottage garden with its crazy paving and its tangle of roses, sunflowers and Michaelmas daisies. Directly opposite, a patch of open ground sloped up to meet the garden of a house on the road above. Jessica studied the back of that house curiously. It was very large and a network of fire-escapes crisscrossed the façade. An hotel, perhaps.

Matthew came in with the breakfast tray. 'You shouldn't be standing, darling.'

She held down a spurt of irritation. He was, after all, taking care of her. 'I'm all right, I've got the crutches.'

Her resentment may have reached him, for he said softly, 'You know the first things about you that attracted me? That gorgeous husky voice and the way you moved—like a dancer. It can't be easy, having to hobble on two sticks.'

Jessica lowered herself into a chair. 'Oh, I shan't waste this. I'll work on the role of invalid till I've got it perfect. The part may come up one day.'

Matthew poured some orange juice. 'It must be useful, being able to file experiences for future use. I suppose novelists do it, too.'

'Whereas you, poor love, are stuck with the material you're offered!'

He smiled. 'With the Sandons, that's colourful enough.'

'Tell me about them.'

'Dominic and I were at Cambridge together. We weren't close, but we met at parties and so on. When he read my biography of the Barretts last year, he got in touch and asked if I'd consider one on his family. They came over with the Conqueror—"Sans-dents", originally, which I'd have thought they'd want to keep quiet about!'

'Not an impressive soubriquet. But you hadn't met his family till last week?'

'I knew his brother, Leo. He's unmarried and lives with them at the Hall, as does their mother, Lady Alice.'

'How gloriously feudal! And his wife doesn't mind?'

'Not in the least. She's French, and accepts that *noblesse oblige*. There are also three sons in their late teens—quite a *ménage*.'

'And they live there all the year round?'

Matthew gave a short laugh. 'Don't sound so incredulous! They have a place in London, but this is their base. Dom's a conscientious landowner and takes a great interest in the estate.'

'And what's the French wife like?'

'Charming. I'm sure you'll like her.'

'I'll be summoned to meet them, then?'

'Invited's the word. I believe they're fans of yours.' He folded his napkin, glancing at her empty plate. 'I'll take these things out of your way while you dress. Can you manage?'

'Yes, darling, thank you.'

She knew, despite his matter-of-factness, that the domestic trivia irked him. After a summer free from writing, during which they had met and married, he was anxious to get back to work. The last thing he needed was a wife unable even to wash the dishes.

The telephone shrilled suddenly on the bedside table and she lifted it. A voice said quickly, 'Freda? It's Charles. Where the hell have you been? I've been trying to get you for days.'

'I'm sorry,' Jessica said, 'we're new here. I'm afraid—'

The phone clicked abruptly and the dialling tone bleeped in her ear. She lowered the receiver, staring at it with raised eyebrow. Then, with a little bang, she replaced it on its cradle. 'Charming old-world courtesy!' she said aloud.

Matthew's voice called up the stairs. 'Was that the phone? I had the water running.'

'For our landlady, I presume. He didn't wait for explanations.'

Slowly and with difficulty she washed and dressed. This was the worst time, she assured herself. In a week or two, things would be much easier. Thank God she'd be mobile before rehearsals started.

She eased herself on to the dressing-stool and critically studied her reflection. Her dark hair, expertly shaped to her head, would have to fend for itself till her return to London. She'd no intention of letting a village hairdresser loose with a pair of scissors. For the rest, high cheekbones, wide expressive mouth, clear skin which, offstage, required the minimum of make-up; and, beneath finely arched brows, those large eyes, a smoky shade between slate and blue, which gave her face in repose a brooding quality. It was good material to work with, she thought impersonally, and repaid the care she gave it.

Plunging her fingers into the jar of skinfood, she began her daily massage.

*

Carrie said nervously, 'Good morning. I—I saw the car, and wondered if Mrs Cowley was back?'

'I'm afraid not,' Matthew replied. 'My wife and I have taken the cottage for a month.'

'A *month*?' She stared at him in bewilderment. 'But I don't understand. She never said she was going away.'

'Unfortunately I can't help you. We dealt directly with the agents.'

'They might know something, Matthew,' Jessica called from the sofa. 'What was their name—Bayliss?'

'Oh, I don't want to bother anyone,' their visitor said hastily. 'It's just that it's awkward, not knowing how long I've got. She's always told me before, so I can fill in if I want to, while she's away. There are always ladies asking.' Seeing Matthew's blank expression, she added, 'I clean for her, you see, two mornings a week.'

His face cleared. 'Then you're just the person we're looking for. Could we take you over? Come inside for a moment and we can discuss it.' He stepped aside and she came diffidently into the room. Matthew said easily, 'Our name is Selby, and you're—?'

'Speight, Carrie Speight.' She smiled shyly at Jessica, and her eyes rested briefly on the plastered leg. She'd a pleasant face, Jessica thought, almost pretty when she smiled, with large, gentle eyes and a childishly full mouth. Her hair looked youthful too, caught back in the nape of her neck. At Matthew's gesture, she perched on the edge of a chair.

'As you see,' he continued, 'my wife isn't able to look after us at the moment.' He made it sound, thought Jessica, amused, as if she normally spent her life scrubbing floors. 'How much time could you spare us?'

'Well, sir, like I said, I come to Mrs Cowley two mornings, Tuesdays and Fridays.'

'It's Tuesday today.'

'Yes, sir. That's why I was wondering. I could stay now, if you like.'

'Please, but we really need more than two mornings.'

Carrie turned to Jessica. She was used to dealing with the mistress of the house, and Matthew's command of the interview flustered her.

'You see, mum, I go to Mrs Markham in Upper Westridge Mondays and Thursdays, and to The Willows all day Wednesday.'

'The Willows?'

'The Nursing Home. Well, Residential, they call it. Old people, like. I help there at weekends, too.'

'You lead a busy life, Miss Speight,' Matthew said drily.

'I could cook your supper, though, if that would help, and dinner too, on the mornings I'm here.'

'That's very good of you,' Jessica said in her husky voice. 'Probably after a week or so, I'll be able to do more myself.'

'Yes, mum.' Carrie glanced uncertainly at Matthew, and when he remained silent, stood up. 'Well, I'll make a start, then.' She bestowed her shy smile on them and turned towards the kitchen, more at home in the cottage than they were themselves.

'I didn't ask about references,' Matthew said in a low voice, 'but she must be well-known in the village. I imagine she's honest enough.'

'I'm sure she is, and she's putting herself out for us. You'll be generous, won't you, darling?'

'Of course. Well, since that's satisfactorily settled, I'll get down to a bit of work, if you'll excuse me. Would you like to sit in the garden?'

'Not just yet. I see the paper's come; I'll glance at that first.'

'Then I'll retire to the study.' He bent and kissed her, his eyes already absent-minded, planning his day. Jessica felt a touch of envy, but things could be a great deal worse. At least they had now acquired Carrie Speight.

Nor was it the last time that day she congratulated herself on their acquisition. Having cycled up the hill for provisions, Carrie proved herself both a competent cook and pleasant enough company. Matthew had not emerged from his study, from which an occasional burst of typing erupted, and Jessica, unused to being alone, was glad of someone to talk to. Sitting in the kitchen while Carrie prepared lunch, she questioned her about the village.

'Well, I don't know that a great deal *happens*,' Carrie answered doubtfully. 'I mean, there are concerts at the school and Harvest Supper and cricket matches, but not what you're used to in London, I expect.'

The supreme understatement. 'But what do you do in your spare time?'

Carrie smiled. 'I don't have very much. I like to keep busy. Mostly I just go for walks. But the gentlemen go to the pub—there are three in the village—or to the Cricket Club, and a lot of the ladies play tennis and squash, though I suppose that's not much use to you.'

'Not at the moment, certainly.'

Carrie continued deftly chopping onions. 'How did you hurt your leg?' she asked conversationally.

'I fell down some rocks on holiday. Silly, wasn't it? I spent the rest of the time in hospital, and had to go to another in London when we got back.'

'So you're here for a rest, while it gets better?'

'Not exactly. My husband's writing a history of the Sandon family, and will be using their library for his research. Also, of course, he'll have to interview them and so on, as he collects his information.'

'Oh,' said Carrie, impressed. 'He writes books, does he, your husband?'

'That's right.' Jessica accepted that her own name, if mentioned, would arouse no more recognition than Matthew's. She seldom appeared on television, and Carrie Speight was unlikely to be *au fait* with names from the West End stage. 'You said you worked at the nursing home,' she went on, reverting to village topics. 'Is that the house we can see from here?'

'That's right, mum. Very nice it is, too. They've got their

own furniture, so it really is like home for them, poor old souls. And Matron's such a kind lady.'

Matthew was extracted from the study for lunch, which he and Jessica ate in the living-room. Carrie, who had volunteered to stay and wash the dishes—'to save the gentleman bothering—' had, at Jessica's insistence, shared the meal, though she ate in the kitchen.

'Wasn't it incredible,' Jessica said, sampling the fluffy omelette, 'that she should arrive on the doorstep like that, just when we needed her?'

'Yes, it was very lucky.' Matthew's tone was abstracted and she realized that for him the meal was an interruption, and he was anxious to return to work. Her impression was confirmed when, as soon as he'd finished eating, he excused himself. 'Get Miss Speight to settle you in the garden before she goes. The fresh air will do you good.'

Another task the admirable Miss Speight could relieve him of, Jessica thought, and was ashamed of her bitterness. She must accept that Matthew was as much obsessed by his work as she by hers. She wouldn't care for interruptions if she were rehearsing or learning her lines—which latter task, she reminded herself, she could usefully undertake.

It was therefore in Carrie's company, not her husband's, that she saw the garden for the first time. It was triangular in shape with the house at its apex, and less private than she'd appreciated. To the right, an open fence was all that separated it from a field, while another field lay beyond the wall at the far end. Jessica could see cows grazing there. Unlike the profusion of flowers at the front, here it was mostly grass—little different, in fact, from the land which surrounded it. A lacy conifer stood in the centre, with a rockery at its foot. Three wide, shallow steps led from the back path down to the grass and these, with Carrie hovering anxiously beside her, Jessica carefully negotiated.

'There's not much privacy, is there?'

Carrie smiled. 'It doesn't stop Mrs Cowley sunbathing. "If they want to look, let them!" she says. There are chairs in the garage, and they have footrests. You should be quite comfortable.'

While Carrie went in search of one, Jessica beat the bounds of her temporary home. It took her only a moment to see that in fact there was no privacy at all. The whole garden lay exposed to anyone either in the adjacent field or walking along the road beside it. Momentarily the fact disturbed her. Working as she did in the constant glare of spotlights, her desire for privacy offstage bordered on the neurotic. Still, they'd only be here a month. She must simply echo the garden's owner. 'They see—what see they? Let them see!' she misquoted wryly.

A decorative wrought-iron gate separated the cottage from the garage and gave access to the front. Through this Carrie was now struggling with two folded deckchairs. Perhaps she thought Matthew would be coming out, too. And perhaps, later, he might.

'I'll put it near the fence, out of the shade of the house,' Carrie said, and Jessica bit back an instinctive protest. Yet why skulk behind the house? She was only going to sit and read, after all. Carrie settled her comfortably with her books.

'I'll be back at six to cook your supper,' she promised. Jessica watched her return through the gate, collect her bicycle which was propped against the side of the house, and disappear from sight.

With a sigh, she leant back and closed her eyes. Moving about was such an effort that she was permanently tired at the moment, and the hot sun flowed comfortingly over her. She drifted into sleep, dimly aware of the unaccustomed sounds of the country about her, the bleating of a sheep, surprisingly close at hand, the distant barking of a dog. Once a tractor, rattling along the road, jerked her briefly awake, but the driver, coming from the village, had his back to her, and she slid back into sleep.

When some time later she came awake again, there was a light flashing in her face and, screening her eyes with her hand, she struggled into a more upright position. The sun had moved round and was now behind her shoulder. It must have been shining on a window on the higher road. Jessica's eyes moved along the backs of the houses, the large one which she now knew to be The Willows Residential Home, and the smaller, private houses on either side. She frowned. None of their windows was reflecting the sun— but she suddenly saw what was. Between the houses, in a gap in the hedge on the top road, she caught the flash again. Then, even as she watched, it moved and was gone.

Her heart began a rapid uneven beat. Binoculars? Was that the explanation? Was someone up there spying on her? But why?

Jessica reached hastily for her crutches, but, forgetting Carrie had propped them against the chair for easy access, her groping hand dislodged them and they fell to the ground beyond her reach. She fought off an illogical but none the less enervating wave of panic. She couldn't move! She was a prisoner in her deckchair until Matthew took it into his head to come and see how she was. And who knew, in his present state of absorption, how long that might be? In the meantime she could only sit there, clearly visible to anyone who cared to study her, the red of her dress a bright splash on the green triangle of the garden. Oh Matthew, for God's sake—! And as the desperate plea formed in her head, miraculously the back door opened and he came down the steps towards her.

'Matthew, thank God! There's someone up there, watching me!'

He paused, the sentence he had ready to greet her swept aside. 'Up where? Nonsense, darling! You've been dreaming.'

'The flashing light woke me. Binoculars, I suppose. In that gap in the hedge.'

He followed her pointing finger, scanning the skyline, but the telltale gleam had gone.

'It *was* there,' Jessica repeated stubbornly.

'Perhaps your fame has gone before you. Whoever it was

will no doubt show up, asking for your autograph.' He turned to more pressing matters. 'Darling, Dominic's just phoned. He's looked out some diaries for me, and I'll need to read through them before I go any further. We've arranged that I'll call and collect them after dinner, and we can work out a rough schedule while I'm there. You won't mind, will you? I shan't be very long.'

Jessica shook her head, her attention still on the mysterious light. But Matthew's presence and his normal conversation had dissolved her anxiety. After all, there must be a logical explanation—a car, perhaps, emerging from a driveway on the far side of the road. She looked up with a smile.

'Sorry about the panic. I couldn't reach my crutches and had no way of attracting your attention.'

'Poor sweet! We'll fix you up with a bell to ring when you need me. Now, how about a cup of tea?'

'Lovely, but I'll come in with you. I've had enough of the garden for one afternoon.'

It had been a long, tiring day, and Lois Winter, matron and proprietor of The Willows, was glad she could now relax. Nine-thirty, she noted, glancing at the carriage clock on the mantel. She kicked off her shoes and went to the cabinet. A gin and tonic would revive her. The window of her pleasant sitting-room, on the first floor of the old house, was still wide open, though she must close it soon, or the moths would come in. Not a breath of air stirred in the darkness outside.

She stood in her stocking feet, sipping her drink and looking appreciatively round the room. It always restored her at the end of the day. She loved the gracefully high ceiling, with its white-painted cornice, the heavy brocade curtains and comfortable chairs. Her eyes lingered affectionately on the silver-framed photograph of her dead husband, but there was no sadness in them. Ten years now she'd been alone, but she'd spent them usefully. She enjoyed her life, was fond of, though often exasperated by, her charges, and had some good friends in the village. All in all, she'd been very lucky.

She carried the glass to her favourite chair and sank luxuriously into it. What was on tomorrow? She was too tired to check in her diary, but days at The Willows followed each other in an admirably orderly fashion and one week was much like the next. Tomorrow, as always on Wednesdays, Carrie Speight would be here for the day. She must ask her to give an extra good dust to Mrs Southern's room. Carrie was a favourite with the old lady, who insisted she was the only one who knew how to clean, a claim which didn't endear Mrs Southern to the other helpers.

Lois smiled to herself and sipped her drink. And this was Della's week, too. Once a fortnight, on half-day closing, she came to wash and set the old ladies' hair. It was amazing what a morale-booster her visits proved. Lois often thanked heaven for the Speight sisters. Life at The Willows would not run as smoothly without them.

Out in the garden an owl hooted suddenly, and she shivered. Silly, how that always affected her. She put her glass on the table and went to close the window, pausing for a moment to look down across the garden at Hinckley's Cottage on the lower road. There were lights on. Someone said the Cowley woman had let it for a month. Shrugging, Lois drew the heavy curtains, and as she did so a knock sounded on the door. She turned swiftly, frowning. It was a strict rule that, once off-duty, she was only to be called in emergency, and a swift recap of the patients, all of whom she'd seen within the last half-hour, brought no imminent crisis to mind.

'Who's there?'

'It's Sister, Matron.'

Lois's frown deepened. Frances had gone off duty over an hour ago; what was she doing back again? 'Is it urgent?'

'I'm afraid so, yes.'

'Very well. Come in.'

Lois walked back to the fireplace and slipped into her shoes. Frances Daly was her second-in-command, a competent woman, divorced and in her late thirties. She wouldn't disturb her unnecessarily. The woman came into the room, turning to close the door behind her, and Lois felt a sudden flicker of unease. Something, she knew instinctively, was very wrong.

'What is it, Frances?' In the privacy of this room, they were on first-name terms.

The woman moistened her lips. She was pale, but her eyes met Lois's steadily. 'There's no easy way to say this. I've been raped.'

Lois came slowly out of her chair, eyes widening in horror. '*What?*'

'I wasn't going to tell you.' Frances spoke jerkily. 'I felt I couldn't bear anyone to know. It's so—degrading.'

'Sit down.' Lois moved swiftly back to the cabinet, poured brandy into a glass, and handed it to her subordinate. 'Drink this.'

Frances sipped at it. She'd started to shake, and held the glass with both hands to prevent it spilling. 'It was horrible,' she said in a low voice. 'I can't tell you—'

'But you will,' Lois insisted gently. 'To start with, where and when did it happen?'

'In the garden, as I was going off-duty.'

'*Our* garden?' Lois felt in the midst of nightmare.

Frances nodded. 'I didn't see him. He caught hold of me from behind and tied my hands behind my back. Then he slipped something over my head—a woolly, helmet kind of thing. And it was dark anyway.' She took another drink, her teeth rattling against the glass.

'I just can't take this in. It must have been—what?—an hour and a half ago?'

'Yes. As I said, I'd decided not to say anything. All I wanted to do was hide. When he left me, I staggered back to the annexe and had a bath—as hot as I could bear it. I felt—defiled.' She was silent for a moment, but Lois could think of nothing to say, and eventually she continued. 'But then I started thinking, suppose it had been Jane, or young Pammy? And it could be, the next time, if I kept quiet. Or anyone else in the village, come to that.'

Lois leant forward. 'Fran love, I know it's painful, but tell me as much as you can. Surely you got some impression of him—height, or build?'

She shook her head. 'Nothing. With my hands tied I couldn't even feel his clothes.' She shuddered, not looking at her friend. 'The worst part of all,' she added, only just above a whisper, 'was that he made me recite nursery rhymes, all the time he—all the time.'

'Oh God!' Lois breathed.

'"Another!" he kept saying. "Go on, you know plenty more!"'

'But that's—obscene!'

'Yes.' Frances dropped her glass on the table with a clatter and put her face in her hands. Lois slipped to the rug, her arms going round her. 'There, love, it's all right, it's over now.'

'But it isn't,' Frances said in a muffled voice. 'I know what happens in cases like this. I'll have to go over it again and again, to the police. And they might not believe me, anyway.'

'They'll believe you,' Lois promised grimly. Frances removed her hands and folded them in her lap, a precarious calm restored. Lois sat back on her heels. 'I can't imagine who it could be. We know most of the people round here, and I can't think—'

'Oh, he probably came from The Packhorse. There was a darts match tonight, and cars parked all along the road. Probably he celebrated too well—or drowned his sorrows —and wandered down the road till he reached us.'

'In which case he's probably gone home now, God knows where.'

'And good riddance.'

'Don't you want him caught?'

'Not really. I never want to see or hear anything of him again.'

There was a silence, during which Lois refilled both their glasses. 'I'll have to get on to Ted Frost,' she said at last.

'I was afraid you'd say that.'

'There's probably no chance whatever of catching him, but it will have to be reported.'

It was hard to know who was the more embarrassed, the red-faced police constable or the victim. In nearly thirty years on the Force, this was the first rape he'd come up against. Fervently he hoped it would be the last. And to a nice, respectable lady like Mrs Daly; it didn't bear thinking about. Stolidly he wrote down what she had to say while Matron stood at the fireplace, gazing into the empty grate.

'Right, ma'am,' he said at last, closing his notebook with relief. 'I'll have to get on to Shillingham, and I'm afraid they'll have more questions. In the meantime, we'll ask Dr Prentiss to come and have a look at you. May I use your phone?' Nursery rhymes, indeed. He'd never feel the same about them again.

As he lifted the receiver, Lois looked at her friend with helpless apology. Shakily Frances smiled back, lifting her shoulders in a gesture of resignation. As she had known would happen, the matter had been taken out of their hands. From now on, she would be a case on the files of Shillingham CID.

CHAPTER 3

Detective Chief Inspector Webb stood in the grounds of The Willows and looked about him. If there was one crime he disliked above others, it was rape. Not only for the terror and humiliation it caused, but for the difficulties posed in following it through. Scenes of Crime had finished photo-graphing the area and were now engaged in gathering samples of soil, leaves and grass from the spot where the alleged crime took place.

Webb pulled himself up. 'Alleged'. Was that a male reaction? He hoped not. In his own mind, he was sure the victim had spoken the truth. She seemed a decent woman, divorced and with no current men friends. According to Mrs Winter, she was reserved, efficient and reliable. Webb accepted that she had reported the matter only from a sense of duty, to prevent a recurrence. Certainly her initial actions bore out her first intention of keeping quiet. Dick Hodges had not reacted well to being told that all the clothes she'd worn at the time had been bundled straight into the washing machine. She had also, by her own account, scrubbed herself all over and washed her hair. Any worthwhile evidence had probably long since been washed away into the Westridge drains.

'Hell and damnation!' Dick had exploded. 'Why didn't she bulldoze the garden, while she was at it?'

Webb sighed and studied the terrain. A close-board fence separated the front and back gardens, but at each side of the house a gate gave access, and he'd established that these were not locked until the off-duty nurses returned from their evenings out. They'd still been unlatched when he arrived the previous evening.

A glass sunlounge had been built against the back of the house—empty at the moment, since Matron had decreed that those showing a prurient interest in police activity should at least be denied a grandstand view. He was aware, however, that their every movement was being watched from the upper windows.

On his far right, conveniently close to the kitchen, was a thriving vegetable garden and beyond it a small orchard of apple trees. In the centre, separating him from his col-leagues, lay a large circular rose-bed. The garden sloped away for some hundred and fifty feet, and at the far end, screened from the lower road by a clump of trees, was the annexe, used as the nurses' home.

According to Frances Daly's statement, she had left the house by way of the sunlounge just after eight o'clock. The path she'd taken, along the left-hand side of the grounds, was bordered by a mass of overgrown shrubs among which, presumably, her attacker had lain hidden. Nearer the annexe, these merged with the fringe of trees on to which the bungalow backed. The spot where the attack had taken place was a small gap just inside the shrubbery, screened from casual observers by a curtain of buddleia. Whether by chance or design, it was sited just beyond the point where light from the house windows would floodlight the garden, yet outside the radius of that from the annexe.

There were two male residents at The Willows, both infirm and in their eighties. Webb felt he could safely discount them from his suspicions. The only other man on the premises was the cook's husband, Frank Chitty, who acted as gardener, odd-job man and porter. They had a basement flat in the main building. According to his statement, he'd gone along to The Packhorse to watch the darts match. A large man, pasty-faced and balding, he'd looked scared, but that might simply have been due to police questioning.

Webb thought back to his meeting with the victim. She'd looked up quickly when he introduced himself and he'd seen recognition in her eyes, though she'd made no comment. Her own name also seemed familiar, but he couldn't place it, and he was sure he hadn't seen her before. He'd a good memory for faces—he needed it.

'I thought I'd at least be spared identification,' she had begun bitterly, and, cutting short his assurances, added: 'You've arranged for a search of the grounds at first light. Once people know where the attack took place, it won't take long to discover who was involved.'

She was right, of course. He'd left her with Sally Pierce, to whom, her protest made, she had presented her story

with almost unnatural calm. Webb had played back the
recording in the car.

'He came up behind me and something sharp pricked my
neck. "Don't make a sound," he said, "or it will be your
last."'

'Would you know his voice again?' Sally'd interrupted.

'No, he was whispering. You can't recognize a whisper.'

'Go on.'

'He told me to put my hands behind my back. He laid
the knife on the ground while he tied them, but I was too
frightened to try to break away. Then this thick, woolly
helmet thing came over my head and he pushed me ahead
of him into the bushes.' She paused. 'It was most effective,
that helmet. Not only could I not see, it dulled all my other
senses, too. I even had difficulty breathing. But I *think* that
when he first came up to me, I caught a whiff of beer on his
breath. I know I immediately thought of The Packhorse,
because I'd seen all the cars along the road.'

She drew a deep breath. 'I imagine you don't want the
clinical details. They can't vary much from case to case.'

'It would help to know if he was violent, apart from
threatening you with the knife.'

'Not physically, no. Mind you, when I knew it was
inevitable I didn't struggle. But the odd thing was he insisted
I kept reciting nursery rhymes.'

'*Nursery rhymes?*'

'It was—macabre. He had the knife in his hand, and it
was an effective prompter, I can tell you. Every time I
faltered, he gave me a little prick. Then, when he'd finished,
he made me turn on my face while he untied my hands and
removed the helmet. He threatened various obscenities if I
turned to look at him, but he needn't have worried.' Her
voice shook momentarily and she steadied it. 'And that,
Miss Pierce, is all.'

So there it was. A weird one, all right, but to Webb's
mind the whiff of beer was the most significant factor. In
all probability it was a one-off occurrence, a combination of

drink and suddenly aroused desire. Say someone from the pub had wandered out for some fresh air and suddenly needed to relieve himself. The road was well lit at that point, and perhaps the dark gardens of The Willows offered the necessary privacy. Then, if he'd seen a woman walking towards him—Webb shrugged. If he was right, the offender was most likely a stranger to the area; a villager would have known where to go if caught short. Anyway, Jackson was at the pub at the moment, obtaining the names of last night's clients, in so far as the landlord could supply them. The list could be checked against that supplied by Frank Chitty. And the visiting darts team—from Oxbury—would have to be seen, but they'd little to go on.

Sally Pierce came up, red hair glinting in the sunshine. 'Right, sir. I've spoken to all the residents whose rooms are at the back. Without exception, they were watching TV at the crucial time.'

'I expected nothing more. None of the neighbours noticed anything, either. People usually draw the curtains once it gets dark. Right, Sally, I want another word with PC Frost. He'll know of any likely villains in the area.'

The search of the grounds was in full swing when, at eight o'clock, Matthew drew back the bedroom curtains. 'What the hell's going on up there?' he exclaimed. 'Must have been a break-in or something—the place is swarming with cops.'

Jessica struggled into a sitting position. 'What are they doing?'

'Crawling about on their hands and knees, from what I can see, but that clump of trees blocks the view.'

'Help me out of bed, darling—I want to look.'

He drew a chair up to the window for her and they watched for some moments before Matthew turned away. 'No doubt it'll be all round the village, whatever it is, so we'll hear in due course. In the meantime I'll get our breakfast.'

By the time he returned with the tray, Jessica too had lost

interest. 'Carrie'll tell us, when she comes to cook supper,'
she said, and her thoughts moved to more personal matters.
'What shall I wear for dinner tomorrow? I haven't dined
with an earl before.'
'Whatever you're comfortable in. It won't be formal.'
'Will they all be there?'
Matthew smiled. 'Gauging the size of the audience? I'm
not sure about the boys, but Dom said Leo and Lady
Alice would be joining us. Leo wasn't around last night—
composing a poem somewhere, no doubt. He's given to long,
rambling verse which no one understands.'
'Has he published any of it?'
'He hasn't even tried. Insists it's for his own satisfaction.
He's a bit of an oddity, but quite harmless. There's a weak
strain in the family which pops up every so often, though it
sometimes skips a generation.'
'Darling, how intriguing! What sort of weakness?'
'Oh, several of them have died young. One in the last
century drowned himself. A bit unbalanced, that's all—
nothing to worry about. And from all accounts, even the
dotty ones are utterly charming.'
'If my family history was full of weirdos, I shouldn't want
to broadcast the fact.'
'Darling, they're proud of it. Proves their blue blood, and
all that. Did I tell you they have the same Christian names
in every generation? Tradition decrees the first son should
be christened Dominic, the second Leo and the third
Jocelyn. No doubt provisions are also made further down
the scale.'
'And you say there are three sons. Isn't it confusing, with
a Dominic and Leo already in the house?'
'They get round it by calling young Dominic Nick and
young Leo by his second name, Patrick. Jocelyn refuses to
answer to anything but Joss, and who can blame him?'
'True, though I like it for a girl. I take my hat off to
Madame la Comtesse. It must take nerve, marrying into a
family like that.'

'Quite the contrary. I mentioned the Sandon charm, and Dom has more than his fair share. Believe me, they were queuing for the honour. And he's not the first this century to choose a French wife. His grandmother was a Mademoiselle Yvette de Chauvigny. It was her diaries Dom handed over last night.'

Jessica smiled. 'How's your French?'

'Just about up to it, except for the abbreviations. I need a code-breaker for those.'

'Will Madame Giselle help you?'

'She offered, but I don't want to impose too much. We'll see how it goes.'

Jessica folded her napkin. 'I'm looking forward to meeting your Sandons,' she said.

Lois looked at the younger woman with concern. For a moment, she'd thought she was going to faint. 'It's all right, Carrie,' she said gently, 'don't worry about it.' Just as well she'd broken the news herself, rather than let her hear a lurid version in the kitchens. Carrie was a sensitive girl.

'They—haven't caught him?'

'No, but I'm sure they will,' Lois said firmly. 'It's not likely to happen again. All the same, don't walk home alone from your baby-sitting for a while. I'm sure someone would always run you back, in the circumstances. Right,' she ended briskly, 'off you go, then. Oh, and Carrie—' the girl turned back, her hand on the doorknob—'go and pacify Mrs Southern, would you? She's been asking for you. Dust on her dresser, no less!'

Carrie's tension dissolved in a smile. 'I'll start with her room, then.'

It was two doors down from Matron's, on the first floor and, like hers, overlooking the back garden. The old lady was, as usual, seated in her chair at the window, a rug over her knees. She turned as the door opened.

'Ah, Carrie. Good morning. You know what's going on down there?' She nodded towards the garden—the only movement, Carrie realized with sympathy, that she could make unaided.

'Someone was—waylaid last night, Mrs Southern.' She didn't want to cause alarm.

'Waylaid? How do you mean?'

'Attacked,' Carrie elaborated unwillingly, moving the ornaments off the dresser.

'*Murdered*, you mean?'

'Oh no, just—attacked. She wasn't—badly hurt.'

'Who was it, do you know?' Carrie shook her head. 'I can't think what the place is coming to, a respectable village like this. The man was drunk, I suppose, or on drugs. From what I read, everyone seems to be, these days.'

Carrie said deliberately, 'I'm going to polish all your furniture this morning, make it shine till I can see my face in it. It's so lovely when it's all gleaming.'

The old face softened, the lines of displeasure fading. 'You're a good girl, Carrie. The only one here who knows how to care for nice things. That Ivy's useless. All she does is move the dust about a bit. Now, what other news have you for me?'

'Let's see. Mrs Cowley's gone off on holiday and a lady and gentleman are at Hinckley's while she's away. The gentleman's a writer. He's doing a story about the Sandons up at the Hall.'

'That's interesting. What's his name?'

'Mr Selby. His wife's a lovely lady, but her leg's in plaster at the moment. She fell while they were away on holiday.' She chatted on for a while, breathing in the fragrant smell of the polish as she rubbed it over the wood, but she was no longer holding her audience. A frown between her eyes, Mrs Southern was staring down at the useless hands on her lap.

Carrie broke off and moved towards her. 'Is something wrong, Mrs Southern? Anything I can get you?'

The sharp old eyes came up to hers, but their expression was uncertain. 'You'll tell me the truth, won't you, Carrie? Is it, or is it not, Christmas?'

Carrie, trying to keep the surprise off her face, answered levelly, 'No, Mrs Southern. Today's the twelfth of September.'

For a moment the grey eyes held hers, before dropping away. 'Then why are people dressing as Santa Claus?' the old lady demanded querulously. And to that, Carrie could find no reply.

Frances had insisted on carrying on with her duties. She was seated in the little office off the hall, reading the mail as she did every morning. Now and again, however, her hand would tremble and she'd have to wait for the spasm to pass. And her mind kept wandering.

So that was Dave Webb. She'd never expected to meet him, things being as they were, and least of all in these circumstances. He'd been gentle with her, though. Not like some detectives she'd heard of.

Heavy footsteps sounded on the marble floor outside and Frank Chitty hesitated on the threshold with an anxious smile, before coming into the office bearing a cup and saucer. 'Cook thought you'd like some coffee, Sister.' Frances had never heard him use his wife's name. 'Feeling all right, are you?'

'Perfectly, thank you, Chitty.' Damn him, she thought with impotent rage, he knows I was the one. They *all* do. She forced herself to add, 'Thank you, it's very welcome.'

He nodded and ambled off. Frances lifted the cup and stopped suddenly with it half way to her mouth. Could it have been *Chitty*? She tried to cloak him with such characteristics as she'd gleaned of her attacker—the soft whisper, the beery breath, the unspeakable hands. She shuddered uncontrollably, and the coffee spilt on her papers. Carefully she set the cup down and mopped up the droplets with her handkerchief. Was this how it was going to be from now on? Would she instinctively cast every man she saw in the role of prospective rapist? And almost harder to bear was the solicitous pity of her colleagues, from Lois all the way down to Cook. Everyone she'd seen this morning had, in the first instance, looked quickly away, not meeting her eyes. Did they privately wonder if it was her own fault, if she'd encouraged him? Did they ask themselves if quiet, reserved Sister had made an assignation in the dark garden, and simply got more than she bargained for?

A sob rose in her throat and she turned it into a cough. Then, with great deliberation, she drank the hot coffee sip by sip, letting it scald her tongue. *He went by the south and burnt his mouth—*

Blindly, she reached for the next letter, slamming her mind shut to everything else.

Della Speight took her white overall out of the carrier-bag and shrugged it on. 'I hear there's been some excitement up here this morning.'

'You could call it that,' Nurse Ellis said shortly. Though unable to explain why, she didn't care for Della.

'A rape, they're saying in the village.'

Obstinately the nurse refused to be drawn. It was natural for Della to be curious, but a bit of tact wouldn't have gone amiss. Damn it, she, Jane, might have been the victim.

Carrie came into the staff-room with a pile of magazines. 'Mrs Pemberton's finished with these. She says we can have them.' She glanced at Della, hesitated, then added, 'Mrs Hathaway's ready, when you are.'

'I was asking Jane about the rape, but she's playing dumb.'

Carrie said in a low voice, 'We don't want to talk about it, Della. Not here.'

Jane Ellis looked from one to the other. The resemblance between them was only superficial, and of the two, Della was the more attractive. She was taller than Carrie, and though her hair was the same colour, it was curly and her eyes were blue. But she hadn't Carrie's gentle willingness, and Jane much preferred her sister.

'All right, keep your secrets,' Della said briskly. 'Mrs

Hathaway, here I come! What will it be today, I wonder—highlighting? Perm? Afro cut?' Mrs Hathaway, at ninety, had hardly any hair at all. With a laugh at her sally, Della went out of the room.

Jane said awkwardly, 'There's no reason why she shouldn't know, of course. Everyone will, soon enough.' She hesitated, looking at Carrie's averted head as she flicked through the magazines. 'She was just rather bright and breezy, for the way I feel at the moment.'

Carrie nodded without turning, and after a moment, with a shrug, Jane Ellis followed Della out of the room.

Jessica said, 'You've been at The Willows today? We were wondering what all the fuss was about.'

Carrie said quietly, 'One of the nurses was raped last night.' It was the first time she'd stated the fact plainly, either out loud or to herself, and doing so instantly established it. No further euphemisms would be possible.

Jessica was staring at her in horror. 'Oh God, no! Where?'

'In the garden.'

'Just across the road there? But that's monstrous! We could almost have seen it!'

Matthew said drily, 'Hardly, darling, in the dark, over a wall and from a distance of a good hundred feet.'

Jessica barely spared him a glance. 'When did it happen?'

'About eight o'clock, I think.'

'And is she all right?'

'She seems to be. She was on duty today, as usual.'

'I suppose they haven't caught him?' Carrie shook her head. 'My God, and I thought it was so peaceful in the country!'

Carrie said carefully, 'I've brought you some eggs. We keep chickens—I can bring you as many as you like.'

'Thank you,' Jessica said with an effort. She waited till the kitchen door had closed behind Carrie, then turned to Matthew. 'What do you think of that? Just across the road!

If there's a rapist in the village, I could scarcely be more of a sitting duck!'

Matthew took her hand and shook it gently. 'Now don't start thinking like that. It was probably a silly girl who led a man on and then got frightened. There's no question of any danger to you. And you've a knight in shining armour, don't forget, prepared to defend your honour!'

'Not last night, I hadn't,' Jessica said shortly. 'You weren't in, were you? Suppose he'd come down here, afterwards?'

Matthew dropped her hand. 'The whole reason for coming here was to give me unlimited access to the Hall. If I'm made to feel guilty each time I leave you, I'll get no work done at all.'

Jessica stared at him, a sick feeling in her stomach. They were on the edge of their first quarrel and she wondered, panic-stricken, how to draw back from it. Matthew, too, seemed to sense the widening gulf, for he went on, 'Look, a rapist is by nature an opportunist. If he sees a woman alone he strikes. But he seldom breaks into houses to achieve his ends. You'd be perfectly safe here, with the doors locked.'

He waited for her to speak, and when she didn't, said abruptly, 'We both need a drink.'

She watched him pour them, her hands tightly clenched. She made herself say, 'Yes, of course. I'm sure you're right' and saw some of the tension go out of his shoulders. He came back with her glass and dropped a kiss on top of her head.

'I didn't mean to snap, darling, I'm sorry. I just didn't want you to dramatize things.'

'I can't help it—it's in my blood.'

He gave a short laugh. 'Of course it is! I was forgetting.' He raised his glass. 'To us—and damnation to all rapists!'

'I'll drink to that!' And as they smiled at each other, harmony was restored again.

CHAPTER 4

Webb's phone was ringing as he returned from lunch, and Inspector Crombie had just lifted it. 'The Lab for you.'

'Thanks, Alan.' He slid behind the desk, reaching automatically for pen and paper. 'Webb here.'

'Bad news, I'm afraid, Dave. Your lad's not a secretor. Blood tests won't help.'

Webb swore under his breath. 'Wouldn't you know it? One of the bloody fourteen per cent! Anything else you can give us?'

'You didn't exactly give *us* much,' the scientist returned drily. 'Thank God the local GP knew his stuff. Laundered clothes aren't the most imformative of clues.'

'So short of examining the wardrobe of half Westridge and Oxbury, we've nothing to go on?'

'Sweet FA. Sorry. You got the report on the burnt-out car?'

'Yes, thanks. We traced the owner, but she's away on holiday. Quite a coincidence—she's from Westridge, too.'

'Hope she's enjoying herself without her suitcase. It was in the car.'

Webb frowned. 'We can only suppose it wasn't hers. No doubt the car was nicked from the drive. We heard it was never in the garage.'

'I read the report on your desk,' Crombie said, as Webb replaced the phone. 'Nursery rhymes, forsooth! What do you make of that?'

Webb grinned. 'Oedipus complex? God knows. Just a warped sense of humour, I'd say. Adds fuel to the drunk theory.'

'You reckon it was someone from the pub?'

'Oh, I think so. Access was almost certainly from the front, through one of the side gates. There's a high wall on both sides dividing the garden from those next door, and no evidence of either being scaled. The wall at the far end beyond the annexe is quite low, but because of the angle and the way the ground slopes away at that point, it would be difficult to climb from the other side. By way of shutting the stable door, I've advised Matron to lock the gates after dark, and let nurses returning from their nights out go through the house.'

His phone rang again. 'Front office here, sir. There's a lady to see you. Says it's urgent. A Mrs Susan Farrow.'

Crombie looked up at Webb's indrawn breath, saw his hands tighten on the receiver.

'Could I have that name again, Sergeant?'

'Farrow, sir. Mrs Susan Farrow.'

Several seconds elapsed before Webb said flatly, 'Very well, Sergeant. Get someone to show her up, would you?'

His eyes met Crombie's, and the Inspector was puzzled by the expression in them. Something had knocked old Spiderman for six. 'Want me to make myself scarce?'

'I'd be grateful, Alan. Thanks.'

Crombie passed the Governor's visitor in the outer office, and glanced at her curiously. Tall and slim, casually but well dressed, she seemed as much on edge as the old man. Curiouser and curiouser. He'd suss it out, though. No point being a detective if he couldn't manage that.

PC Dacre knocked on Webb's door and, opening it, stood to one side. Webb said, 'Thank you, Constable.' And, as the door closed behind him, 'Hello, Susan.'

'Dave, I'm sorry to burst in on you like this, but I've just heard about the rape. Have you found out who did it?'

He stared at her blankly. 'The rape?'

'I can't believe it. Fran, of all people. It's so—'

'Fran. Frances Daly—of course. You trained together.'

She looked at him in surprise. 'You mean you didn't realize?'

'During the last five years,' he said heavily, 'I've done my best to forget everything about you. What the hell are you doing here, anyway? The last I heard you were up in Stratford or somewhere.' He gestured to a chair. 'I'm sorry, I'm forgetting my manners. Please sit down.'

She did so, crossing one slim leg over the other. 'I'm temping at the moment. I've signed on at the Nursing Agency.'

'But why here?'

'Why not? You don't own this bloody town, do you? I've as many friends here as you have.'

'Yes, of course.' He couldn't believe this was happening. The bitterness of their divorce had left deep scars. Certainly he'd never expected to be chatting to her over his desk—or anywhere else—ever again. He added with an effort, 'How's Tony?'

Her hands clenched. He saw she was wearing on her little finger the amethyst he'd given her for their fifth anniversary. The sight of it was like a douche of cold water.

'It didn't work out,' she said quietly, her defiance gone. 'He left me a year ago.'

'I'm sorry.'

'Are you?' Her voice was bitter. 'Or do you think it served me right, since he left his first wife for me?'

She looked so exactly the same—he'd never anticipated that. Still the firm, athlete's body, with small high breasts and long legs. Even her hairstyle was unchanged, chin-length in a soft bob, and the clear blue eyes under their straight brows looked as candid and honest as ever. But he'd discovered they could lie. As always, her mouth was the most striking thing about her. Though he knew it was simply that her even, well-shaped teeth were crowded too far forward, when her lips closed over them, they looked full and disconcertingly sensual.

He rubbed a hand over his face. 'Susan, forgive me, but I haven't time for social calls. I've a hell of a lot on.'

'Still the same old Dave!' He was, too. She'd been assessing herself the changes five years had wrought in him, and they were surprisingly few. His thick brown hair was as plentiful as ever and his lean, rangy body hadn't gained an ounce. Possibly his mouth was harder and his eyes more cynical—but she was to blame for that. Interestingly enough, he still attracted her—and she felt it was mutual. Why else was he showing her the door? He hadn't remarried, either. She'd checked on that. 'It wasn't a social call, anyway,' she added. 'If you remember, I asked about the rape.'

'Oh yes. Well, I'm afraid I've no more to tell you than you doubtless read in the papers—or heard from Frances herself.' He'd the uncomfortable feeling she was using it as an excuse. She must have known when she came to Shillingham that she'd bump into him; specially if she was temping at the General, next door to the police station.

She said, not looking at him, 'Could we meet for a drink?'

He forced his voice to remain level. 'I don't think there'd be much point, do you?'

'I won't eat you, you know. It's just that I'd like to think we were still friends.'

'Friends!'

She stood up abruptly. 'All right, you've made your point. Sorry to have taken up your time.'

His chair grated as he too got to his feet. 'Look, Susan, I'm sorry. You caught me on the hop, I don't mind telling you.'

'Then you will meet me?'

'I didn't mean—'

'For old times' sake?'

His phone rang. 'All right, just a drink, if you insist. Now you really must excuse me.' He reached for the phone.

'When?'

'God knows. Give me a ring.' With luck, her pride would prevent her. He put a hand over the mouthpiece. 'Can you find your own way down?'

She nodded. 'Goodbye, Dave.'

He did not reply. Throughout the brief conversation with his superior, his stomach was churning as it had during the days of his marriage. Old times' sake, my eye! They'd been hellish and he'd thought they were behind him. Ridiculous to let her get under his skin again. She'd no claims on him now.

So that creep had left her. Webb hoped he was paying maintenance. Bloody hell, as if he hadn't enough to worry about! He made an angry movement and the draught of it wafted her scent towards him. While she was with him, he'd been unaware of it; now, after her going, it lingered behind to stir old memories.

Somehow, while his mind raced, he'd answered the questions demanded of him. As the Chief Superintendent rang off, he depressed the button and dialled again.

It was against all his rules, phoning from the office, but he had to speak to Hannah. Now. He hadn't seen her for six weeks; she'd been touring Europe with her parents, who were over from Canada. But she'd been due back last night. Surely she'd be—?

'Hello?'

'Hannah! Thank God!'

'Hello, David! Are you home this afternoon?'

'No, I'm at the station.'

'Is anything wrong? You sound a bit strung up.'

'Can I see you this evening?'

'Oh love, I'm sorry. It's my parents' last night—they're flying back tomorrow. Charlotte's here, and we're going out for a meal. She sends her regards, by the way.'

Webb had a brief mental picture of Hannah's aunt in a sunlit square, seconds before its calm was shattered. 'Thanks—mine to her. How about tomorrow, then?'

'Well, I've arranged to see Gwen. With my getting back so late, we haven't had time to go over timetables, and school starts on Monday. Still, it needn't take the whole evening. Would nine o'clock be any good?'

'Fine.' He paused. 'I've missed you.'

'That's nice.' There was surprise in her voice. In their no-strings relationship, they seldom made such admissions. 'You're sure nothing's wrong?'

'Not now.' With Susan sitting opposite him, it had suddenly, appallingly, been as though Hannah were erased from his life, her very existence in doubt; an impression underlined by six weeks' absence.

She said softly, a laugh in her voice, 'As it happens, I missed you, too.'

His spirits rose suddenly. What was he getting so steamed up about? His life with Susan was past. Hannah, thank God, was his present. 'Bless you. Nine o'clock tomorrow, then.'

As he put the phone down, Crombie's inquiring head came round the door. 'OK to come back in?'

Webb laughed, and his remaining unease dissolved. 'Yep, the coast's clear. Now, about that darts team—'

It was cloudy that afternoon, and Jessica did not go into the garden. She still felt exposed there, despite common sense and Matthew's reassurances. Particularly after the rape. Suppose it had been the same man who was watching her, staking out his next victim? She shrugged the thought impatiently aside—but she remained indoors.

Closing her ears to Matthew's erratic typing behind the study door, she settled herself on the sofa and opened her book. And the telephone rang. Fortunately it was within reach.

'Freda—hi! I'm at Heathrow—we've just landed. Smooth flight, thank God, so I didn't need my tranquillizers!'

Jessica wished her landlady had been less secretive about her movements. 'This is Jessica Selby speaking. I'm sorry, but Mrs Cowley isn't here. She's away on holiday.'

'Not there? She must be! I'm coming to visit with her on the weekend.'

Jessica frowned. But at least this caller hadn't rung off in her ear. 'There must be some mistake. My husband and I have the cottage for a month.'

'But this is Wilma Bernstein, from New York! Freda spent her vacation with me last year, and the return visit was

planned then. She called me only two weeks ago with the
final arrangements. I'm to spend two nights in London, and
come out to Broadshire Saturday for two weeks.' A pause,
then, more suspiciously, '*Who* is this?'

'Jessica Selby. I really am sorry, Miss Bernstein, but I
can't help at all. Perhaps she left a forwarding address with
the agents.'

Anger replaced suspicion. 'You're saying I flew three
thousand goddam miles for nothing? What is this? Here I
welcomed Freda into my home—'

'Their name is James Bayliss, in Marlton. Would you like
me to look up their number?'

'I guess so. This is the craziest thing I heard.'

As Jessica scrabbled through the directory, the pips began
their rapid bleeping and the line went dead. She scribbled
down the number in case Miss Bernstcin rang back when
she'd found the right coin, but after a few minutes, deciding
she wasn't going to bother, Jessica returned to her book. It
wasn't her affair, anyway.

'Darling, I've some news for you!'

Guy put his briefcase on the table. 'Not another rape, I
hope.'

'No, good news this time. Interesting, anyway. Remember
that man I saw in the post office? Well, he's Matthew Selby,
the writer. Carrie Speight told me this morning. Even better,
you know who he's married to, don't you?'

'Surprise me.'

'Jessica Randal! Carrie didn't know that bit—who she is,
I mean, but I remember seeing the wedding on TV about
a month ago.'

Their fifteen-year-old daughter was standing in the doorway. 'Jessica Randal, did you say? Here?'

Kathy smiled at her. 'I thought that would interest
you.'

'But how fabulous! Will you ask her round?'

'Oh, come on!' Guy protested. 'They're still more or less

on their honeymoon. The last thing they'll want is to be bothered with star-struck fans.'

'But she's broken her leg, Carrie says, and he's researching the Sandons. I reckon that makes it open season.'

'Then you *will* ask her, Mummy?'

'I don't see why not. It can't be much fun, stuck at home with a broken leg while your new husband hobnobs with the gentry! She'd probably be glad of the invitation.'

Guy's expostulations were lost as his daughter, with a whoop of joy, seized her mother round the waist and waltzed her round the kitchen till they collapsed, laughing, against the table.

'Jessica Randal!' Angie exclaimed again. 'I can't believe it! She used to be married to Howard Kane, didn't she? What's her new husband like?'

'The intellectual type, but attractive. Not as beautiful as Number One, but I bet his IQ would knock Kane's into a cocked hat.'

Guy said pointedly, 'I'm going to cut the grass.'

He was ignored. 'What will you ask them to?' Angie demanded.

'I thought drinks on Saturday.'

'It's pretty short notice. You'll have to invite them straight away.'

'All right, I'll phone now. It'll be Freda's number.'

Angie waited in a fever of excitement while her mother dialled.

'Mrs Selby? You don't know me, but I'm Kathy Markham, from the top road. I heard of your arrival from Carrie Speight.'

'Good evening, Mrs Markham.' Jessica's husky voice came over the line.

'We're having a few friends for drinks on Saturday, and wondered if you could come. We should love to see you, and it'd be a chance to meet your neighbours.'

'How kind of you. We'd be delighted.'

Kathy smiled at her daughter's radiant face. 'That's

marvellous. Six-thirty, then. Ours is the house with the
copper beech at the gate, just past The Willows. We look
forward to meeting you.'

Matthew had come in while Jessica was speaking. 'What
are you letting us in for?' he asked, as she put down the
phone.

'Drinks on Saturday, at the Markhams'. It should be fun.
She'd heard of us through Carrie.'

Matthew smiled. 'The Westridge bush telegraph in person. Right, darling, if you're ready it's time we were leaving
for the Hall. I didn't expect to need an engagement diary
up here, but it seems I was wrong!'

Jessica felt immediately at home. The familiarity of the Hall
surprised her, till she realized it resembled a set she'd once
acted on. And the Sandons could have been characters from
a play, the silver-haired dowager, the elegant Countess—
and particularly the younger brother, Leo. He was tall and
thin, and wore his black hair long, though it had receded to
form an abnormally high forehead. Resplendent in plum-
coloured jacket, frilled shirt and floppy cravat, he sported a
small beard—proof, as Matthew said later, of his poetic
leanings.

By contrast, Lord Sandon was disappointingly conven-
tional. Tall, broad and clear-skinned, he looked more farmer
than earl. But the charm Matthew had spoken of was in his
smile and the warmth of his welcome.

Dinner was served in a magnificent room that could have
seated fifty, and they were waited on by a manservant.

'This is in your honour,' Dominic told Jessica with a
twinkle. 'When we're alone, we use the morning-room.'

'I'm duly impressed!'

'But it is such a pleasure to meet you, Mrs Selby,' the
Countess said in her attractively accented voice. While her
English was correct, it was peppered with French phrases
without any hint of affectation. It was simply that she
thought in both languages, and selected the most apposite

phrase from either. 'We never miss one of your plays. I hope your accident will not keep you off the stage?'

'I don't think so. We're due to start rehearsals at the end of October, by which time I should be completely back to normal.'

'And what is the play?'

'Quite a change for me. Agatha Christie's *Ten Little Niggers*.'

'I do not believe I know that one.'

'It's taken from a nursery rhyme, Giselle,' Leo put in, in his surprisingly deep voice. '"Ten little nigger boys went out to dine. One choked himself to death, and then there were nine."'

'Not a happy quotation while we're dining ourselves!' his mother chided him, and they all laughed.

'My great-grandmother was an actress,' Dominic remarked. 'The old man was one of the stage-door Johnnies who abounded at that time. She was sweetly pretty, from all the portraits, but of course without a thought in her head!'

'*Chéri*—' Lady Sandon interrupted, with an embarrassed glance at her guest, who, however, dissolved into laughter.

'I do beg your pardon! In fact the word actress was a euphemism, she was actually one of the chorus line. But whatever her intellect, my great-grandfather adored her to the end of his life. I'll show you her portrait later. More grist to your mill, Matthew.' He turned back to Jessica. 'Are you comfortably settled in the village? I'd hoped you'd be our guests here, but Matthew didn't care to live over the shop!'

'I entirely agree with him!' Leo declared. 'One needs to escape one's work environment, however pleasant—step back, as it were, and see things in perspective. If one breathes the same atmosphere working and resting, one becomes positively clogged with it.'

As they left the table, Jessica found Leo at her elbow. 'Might I ask you a favour, Jessica? I may call you Jessica, mayn't I, since I've always adored you from afar?'

'Of course,' she murmured, hoping she was assenting to the first name rather than the still-unstated request.

'Might I ask you to read aloud a few of my offerings? To hear you recite them would give me enormous pleasure.'

'Certainly, I'd be most interested to see your work.'

'Splendid! Then if I may, I'll call round in a day or two, and we shall indulge ourselves.'

Over his shoulder, Jessica caught Matthew's quizzically raised eyebrow.

'Is he real?' she demanded, as they were driving home through the woods. 'Does he always proclaim like that?'

'Always. I wondered what was coming when he asked you for a favour. I was on the point of flicking him with my glove and demanding satisfaction.'

'Idiot!' She smiled at him fondly. 'It was an interesting evening, wasn't it? My first brush with the landed gentry; I found it most stimulating.'

Carrie, on her way home from baby-sitting, waited for their car to pass before crossing the road. She didn't know who was inside it, and they hadn't noticed her. As she turned into Donkey Lane, she saw there was a light in the front room. That meant Bob Davis was still there, which was a pity. He stood up as she let herself into the cottage.

''Evening, Carrie. I didn't realize it was so late. We've a cow about to calve and I promised Dad I'd look at her before turning in.' He paused. 'You didn't come home alone, did you? You must be careful, while this maniac's about.'

Matron had said the same thing. 'I hadn't far to come,' she replied.

'Even so . . . Well, I'd best be going.' Bob turned to the door, and as Della made no move to show him out, Carrie opened it for him. 'Thanks for the beer, Della. Good night then.'

Carrie closed the door behind him and turned the key. 'He's in love with you,' she said flatly.

'More fool him.'

'But he's such a nice chap.'

'Look, it's not my fault. I've told him it's no go. If he wants to spend his evenings making eyes at me, that's up to him.'

'But he's been hurt enough, with his wife dying and all.'

'Well, what do you expect me to do about it? He hasn't had any encouragement.'

'You could stop him coming. That would be kindest. It upsets me to see him here, looking all—humble and devoted.'

'Your trouble is you're too sensitive. Now stop going on at me, for Pete's sake. I'm not in the mood for it.'

Carrie sighed. 'You remembered to shut up the hens, didn't you? I don't want a fox getting them.'

'Yes, I shut up your precious hens. I don't know about you, but I'm ready for bed. Do you want to go to the bathroom first?'

'All right.' As Carrie walked through the dark kitchen to the bathroom beyond, she tried to close her mind to other people's troubles. She'd enough of her own.

CHAPTER 5

It was Friday morning. Everyone known to have been at The Packhorse on Wednesday had been interviewed and, with varying degrees of willingness, had agreed to the clothes they'd been wearing being sent for examination. Webb had stressed they'd the right to refuse but as the darts captain remarked, 'Tongues would start wagging if we did.'

Crombie pushed a pile of statements to one side. 'If you ask me, this is the one that got away. Nobody noticed anyone leave, except to go to the men's room, and no one was absent for a suspiciously long time. Of course, our man could have been the inoffensive little chap in the corner that nobody noticed. In fact, he probably was.'

Webb grunted, glancing through his mail. Among the already opened letters, he came across a sealed one marked Personal and slit it open, his eyes rapidly scanning the sheet of paper. Then he said softly, 'Hell and damnation. Listen to this, Alan.

Dear Sir, I've just read in the *News* about the nursery rhyme rape. You might be interested to know I had a similar experience a few years ago. I was too ashamed to report it, and have never mentioned it to anyone, but surely it must be the same man? I too had a hood slipped over my head, my hands tied behind me, and was made to recite nursery rhymes throughout my ordeal. There's nothing to be gained by our meeting, but I thought you should know it's almost certain that the rape you're investigating isn't this man's first.

He looked up, meeting Crombie's eyes. 'A new line in anonymous letters. Good hand, educated woman by the look of it. God, Alan, the percentage of rapes that are never reported! If he's done it once before, he could have done it a dozen times. Far from the one-off we were hoping for, he's turned at a stroke into an habitual offender.'

'No signature at all? Not even "A well-wisher"?'

'Not a damn thing.' Webb slammed his open palm on the desk. 'Whatever she says, of course I have to see her. We need to know exactly when and where it happened before, the method of approach, whether the knife was in evidence —a dozen things.' He flipped over the envelope. 'Postmark's Ashmartin, but that's no help. She could have gone in for the day shopping, or moved house in the meantime.'

'You reckon it's genuine?'

'I wish it wasn't, but it has the ring of truth about it.'

'Put an ad in the *News* asking her to phone you. You needn't actually meet if she's so hell-bent on secrecy, but at least you could question her. And we know she reads the paper, so she must still be in the county.'

'That's a thought. Our only hope, anyway. In the meantime I'll get through to Ashmartin and see if they've anything on their books. I'm not hopeful—if they had, they'd
have been in touch before now.'

It opened a new avenue, anyway, he thought gloomily as
he waited to be connected, but it was one he'd have preferred
to remain closed.

The day proved frustratingly unprofitable, and by nine
o'clock that evening, Webb was pacing up and down his
living-room. His small flat was at the top of a custom-built
block, erected along with several others in the grounds of
gracious old houses which had been demolished to accom-
modate them. Hannah's larger flat was on the floor below,
overlooking the extensive grounds, but his own, at the front,
had a view down the long hill to the town centre. During
the summer it presented a rich, multicoloured foliage of
trees, so dense it seemed he could walk along the tops of
them.

Every evening when he returned home, he spent some
minutes at the window, allowing the physical distance he'd
come from his office to extend to mental dissociation. It was
a useful unwinding procedure, and he'd have been surprised
to learn it was endorsed by the Honourable Leo Sandon.
This evening, however, he'd already been home an hour,
and the greenery of the outlook had merged into darkness
as lights sprang up down the hill.

He had bathed and changed into leisure clothes. Despite
the open window, the room was airless after the day's heat.
Ten past nine. But she'd come as soon as she could. He
knew where he was with Hannah.

When she did arrive, he had the door open before her
finger was off the bell. They stood for a moment looking at
each other, an intangible shyness the legacy of the six-week
separation. She seemed subtly different from his memory of
her, more bronzed from the European sun, her tawny hair
highlighted by its strength. But her grey eyes on his, her

half-smile as she waited for him to speak, ignited the impatience within him. He reached for her hand, drew her gently inside and, with rising urgency, into his arms. And at once his unacknowledged fear that somewhere on her travels she might have met someone else, someone willing to offer her marriage and a family—even that the extended separation might have given her pause to reflect adversely on their own relationship—all these doubts were gloriously swept away by her clinging arms and the answering passion of her mouth.

Their news would have to wait. By unspoken consent they went straight to the bedroom, rediscovering each other with a joy and tenderness that Webb acknowledged humbly he did not deserve. Love was a word he'd erased from his vocabulary since Susan's going. It held too much of pain, vulnerability, dependence. None of these attributes would he seek again. Hannah knew and accepted that. As deputy headmistress of an exclusive girls' school, her career was more important to her than marriage. That they had come together, two people neither asking nor giving more than was acceptable to the other, was a continuing wonder to him, and he fervently thanked whatever fates there were for his good fortune.

When they were lying side by side, fingers tightly linked, she said softly, 'I told you I missed you.'

'I believe you. Thank God.' He lifted her hand in his, kissed her fingers, and said, entirely without premeditation, 'Susan's back.'

She stiffened, her head turning towards him. 'Back where?'

'In Shillingham. She came to see me yesterday.'

Hannah considered this. 'Which was why you phoned?'

'Yes.'

She asked carefully, 'What did she want?'

'Allegedly to speak to me about the rape. A friend of hers was involved.'

'What rape was that?'

'I was forgetting you've not had time to read the papers. There was an incident in Westridge. Rather unpleasant.'

'And your wife came back because of it?'

'No,' he answered quietly, accepting that she had seized unerringly on the fact that most disturbed him. 'She was already here. She's signed on with a nursing agency.' He paused, then added flatly, 'Her husband's left her.'

Hannah digested this in silence. Then she said, 'How did you feel, seeing her again?'

'Churned up. Resentful. Oddly protective. Mixture as before.'

'Where's she living?'

'She didn't say. Nurses' hostel, probably. God knows if she's any money.'

'Darling, you're really not responsible for her.'

'So I keep telling myself.'

'Are you going to see her again?'

'She wants us to have a drink sometime.'

'And you agreed?'

'In a manner of speaking. I said she could give me a buzz.'

Hannah lay gazing at the blue square of the window. At last a faint breeze was stirring, and the curtains moved lazily. Damn Susan. Why did she have to come back and put a spoke in their smoothly-turning wheel? She'd hurt David badly before, she could do so again. Did he want her back? Would he take her, if she asked him?

The idea took solid form as a lump in Hannah's chest. Yet she was being selfish. Perhaps after her unhappy experience, Susan genuinely wanted to try again. Suddenly all the joy of their lovemaking, her excitement at seeing him again, was under threat. She made herself say quietly, 'Would you like me to take a back seat for a while?'

His hand tightened painfully on hers, but when he spoke his voice was light. 'If you can ask that after the last half-hour, I'm a failure!'

Reflectively she stroked his fingers, her eyes still on the

window. Did he know how susceptible he still was to his ex-wife? If Susan were clever, she could play on his protectiveness, his memory of having loved her. And that might just be enough.

'I'm so glad you could come!' Kathy greeted them warmly. 'Darling, here are Mr and Mrs Selby. My husband, Guy.'

'And we're Matthew and Jessica. Forgive me for not shaking hands—I might overbalance!'

'We'll find somewhere comfortable for you, and you can hold court. Everyone's longing to meet you. Especially our daughter, Angie,' she added, as a pretty young girl came hurtling down the stairs. 'She's hoping to get into RADA when she leaves school.'

'We must have a long talk,' Jessica said.

'And this is Mr Selby, Angie,' Kathy prompted, and the girl turned from Jessica long enough to shake his hand.

Matthew's smile was brilliant. 'Angie, did you say? My ex-wife's name, but I shan't hold that against you!'

There was a brief, embarrassed silence, then Kathy gave an uncertain little laugh and led the way to the sitting-room. As they appeared in the doorway, the babble of voices died away and everyone turned to face them. Jessica, used to making an entrance, thankfully slipped into auto-pilot, concealing her surprised hurt at Matthew's rudeness. Was that dart of spite for herself or the child?

It pricked at her memory as she smiled and chatted to the succession of people who came to be introduced, filing names and faces for possible future use. Lois Winter, matron of The Willows, a pleasant woman with a young face and pretty grey hair; the Vicar and Mrs Dugdale; Charles and Annette Palmer—

Charles? Jessica's eyes flicked to his face. 'Haven't we—' she began, and broke off at his warning look. Of course, the man on the telephone! She recovered herself, seeing his flash of gratitude. All the same, he shouldn't escape unscathed for hanging up on her. He was a tall, florid-faced man with a low forehead and crinkly black hair. His wife, pale and blonde, had noticed nothing. Intriguing! Well, he could wriggle on her pin a little longer, though in fairness not in front of his wife.

When all the introductions were over, everyone split into groups again. Lois Winter had taken the seat beside her. 'Does it bore you to speak of your work, or may I say how much I enjoyed *Private Lives*?'

'Please do! I've yet to meet an actor who can refuse a compliment!'

'I hope your injury won't keep you off the stage too long.'

'I don't think so, it's a relatively simple fracture. We hope to open at the Embassy in mid-November, in *Ten Little Niggers*.'

A frisson passed over her companion's face, but Jessica, who hadn't read the *Broadshire News*, did not interpret it. The national press had afforded the rape only a small inside paragraph, and no mention had been made of nursery rhymes.

'May I wish you a long and successful run, then,' Lois said steadily. 'I'm also a fan of your husband's. I've read all his books and admire them tremendously,'

Matthew himself, ashamed of his outburst, had nevertheless watched the obeisance paid to his wife with sour envy. He'd have to accept TV offers after all, he mocked himself. Only then would be become familiar to the square-eyed public. He found himself chatting to the local headmaster, a hollow-cheeked and sad-eyed man with dull, dusty-looking hair. His wife was small and plump, her face unashamedly devoid of make-up and her pronounced north-country accent at variance with the soft local burr to which Matthew had already become accustomed. Her husband's origin was apparent only in the occasional flattening of a vowel, a southern university having for the most part standardized his accent.

'A fine Yorkshire name you have there, Mr Selby,' Mrs Bakewell was saying.

'I suppose it is.' Never having thought about it, Matthew was vaguely surprised.

'Grand part of the country. We'll be glad to get back there, when Donald retires.'

Her husband gave a brief smile, and Matthew wondered if Bakewell himself had other ideas. He'd an air of disappointment about him; perhaps there'd been hopes of a professorship, and he resented ending his career a village schoolmaster.

'I hear you're doing a history of the Sandon family, Mr Selby,' Donald Bakewell remarked. 'Lot of black sheep there, I imagine. All safely in the past, of course. I don't know the present earl, but he's highly thought of in these parts. Looks after his employees well, from all accounts.'

'We met at Cambridge,' Matthew said, and, seeing Mrs Bakewell's lips tighten, regretted the admission. No doubt Leeds or Bradford would have been a more acceptable academe. 'They have quite a colourful past, but I dare say that goes for most of our old families.'

'Have you been to the church yet? Reg Dugdale has registers going right back, and the graveyard's full of Sandons. The earliest tombstones are illegible, more's the pity, but if you peer close enough you can make out a few thirteen hundreds. The family still has boxed pews, you know, which they dutifully occupy at Christmas, Easter and Harvest Thanksgiving, though I believe the present countess is Catholic.'

'I suppose all the Sandons were, once, coming from French stock,' put in a pale, fair woman who had drifted up and stood listening to the conversation.

'So were we all, once, Mrs Palmer!' the schoolmaster reminded her. 'Our little church switched faiths along with the others, when it was expedient to do so.'

'Of course—I was forgetting.' The newcomer flushed and Matthew felt sorry for her. He turned as an attractive woman joined them, and learned with gratitude that she had read his books. Perhaps this wasn't such a backwater after all!

Jessica meanwhile, with her usual flair for timing, chose her moment to tease Charles Palmer. Aware of him still on the fringe of the group nearest her, she looked up at her hostess and said in her clear, carrying voice, 'Tell me about Freda Cowley. Her departure seems to have taken people by surprise.'

'Yes, she didn't even tell Carrie, which was thoughtless. But she's always been impulsive. Probably the chance suddenly came to go off for a week or two, so off she went.'

'I had a decidedly odd phone-call,' Jessica went on, and, noting Charles Palmer's rigidity from the corner of her eye, used a dramatic pause to maximum effect. 'A woman over from the States,' she continued then, 'who seemed to think Mrs Cowley was expecting her. She'd been invited to spend her vacation at Hinckley's Cottage.'

Kathy frowned. 'That's too bad. Freda's gone too far this time. What did you tell her?'

'I offered to give her the estate agents' number, but her money ran out while I was looking it up and she didn't ring back.'

'It would be Wilma Bernstein, I expect. Freda said she was coming, but I didn't know when.'

A few minutes later, when the groups had reformed, Jessica found Charles Palmer bending over her to refill her glass.

'Your revenge was masterly. Please forgive my rudeness on the phone, but you'll appreciate my alarm at an unknown voice, specially when I'd foolishly identified myself.'

Jessica sipped her drink thoughtfully. 'Have you a pair of binoculars, Mr Palmer?'

'What an odd question! No, why?'

'It doesn't matter.' She was a good judge of acting and felt he spoke the truth. Nevertheless, she didn't care for him, and when someone else came to speak to her and Palmer moved away, she wasn't sorry to see him go. Meanwhile

Matthew, who hadn't been near her since their arrival, was also approaching.

'I think we should be going, darling. Carrie will have supper ready.' He wasn't quite meeting her eye, and Jessica felt a surge of irritated affection. She loved him dearly, but she was finding he could annoy her. The honeymoon was over!

When they made their farewells, Angie was standing at her mother's side. Mindful of the initial embarrassment, Jessica said impulsively, 'We didn't have our talk, did we? How about coming round for coffee? I'll phone in a day or two.' The child's delight was evident, and Jessica's conscience assuaged.

'I gather I'm still in disgrace?' Matthew commented as he helped her into the car.

'Is that why you've been avoiding me?'

'I couldn't get within yards of you. But I am sorry, darling. I behaved badly.'

'Why?'

He smiled ruefully 'Pique, I suppose. It was so obviously you they wanted to meet. I was the also-ran.' He brushed aside her protest. 'You must remember that last time I was married, I was the family celebrity. I still haven't adjusted to second fiddle.'

'That's ridiculous, as you well know. In many circles, you're better known than I am. People can read your books anywhere; they only see me act in London.'

'They know you here, all right. Am I forgiven, then?'

'Of course. Now, tell me what you thought of everyone.'

'Spider? Fleming here. Sorry to interrupt your Sunday, but there's been a development.'

Webb swore silently. He'd been about to drive out to a new site he'd discovered, to do some sketching. 'What kind of development, sir?'

'This nursery rhyme business. We've a body that seems to tie in. See you in twenty minutes.' And he rang off.

A *body*? That was all he needed. Stuffing his notebook into his pocket, Webb pulled the door of his flat shut and ran down the two flights of stairs. He hadn't contacted Jackson —perhaps the Chief Super had. But Jackson was a family man, and less likely to be home on Sunday afternoons. He was probably in the park with Millie and the kids.

Webb wove his way between the leisurely Sunday drivers, curbing his impatience. Once on the Broadminster road, he made better time. How could a body tie in with the nursery rhymes? The case was escalating, he thought uneasily. First the anonymous letter, now this. And they'd made no head-way at all on the rape.

County Headquarters was a large and impressive building in the Broadshire countryside. There was no village nearby, but an old stone bridge that crossed the river just down the road had given the area its name. Webb turned off the main road, drove round to the car park. The day was heavy and still, a sulphur light over everywhere. It would probably thunder later—clear the air a bit.

Fleming was in his office, with Eric Stapleton. The pathologist always depressed Webb, not only because he was unavoidably associated with death, but because of the dried-out air about him, as though all his natural juices had been sucked dry. The expression in the small eyes behind their rimless glasses never altered. They were surprised at nothing.

'Sit down, Spider. What do you make of this?' Fleming pushed across the desk a plastic envelope inside which was a crumpled piece of paper. On it, several lines of verse were neatly typed. Webb read them, his heart sinking. '*Here comes a candle to light you to bed, And here comes a chopper to chop—off —your—head.*'

'Except,' said Fleming drily, 'that her head wasn't chopped off. She was suffocated, Stapleton tells me, prob-ably with a pillow. And this was stuffed in the pocket of her dress.'

'Where was the body found, sir?'

'In a dried-up ditch off the Heatherton–Marlton road.'

'No ID on her, I suppose?'

'Right. Woman in her late thirties, quite attractive—or she would have been. Height five foot six, weight nine stone, hair dyed blonde, eyes blue. No distinguishing marks.'

'I'll check with Missing Persons. How long has she been dead?'

Stapleton spoke for the first time. 'Tell me when she was last seen, and I'll hazard a guess!'

'Roughly, sir?'

'Judging by the maggots, about ten days.'

'From which you'll gather we can't issue a photograph. So have a quick look at her, Spider, and do one of your artist's impressions to pass to the press. At the very least, it'll give an idea of her hairstyle and the shape of her face. Someone might come forward.'

Webb grimaced. 'Hope my Sunday lunch stays down.'

'Sorry, but you're the best artist we have. Saw one of your cartoons in the *Weekly News*. Damn good.'

'Thank you, sir. Mike Romilly twists my arm every now and then.'

Half an hour later, his visit to the dead thankfully behind him, Webb sat at his desk drawing his impression of her. His forte lay in cartoons and landscapes; his portraiture was less certain, but he was doing his best, and under his pencil the dead face was coming alive. He could only hope the resemblance was sufficiently strong for someone to recognize her.

And someone did. With the introduction of murder, the national press showed more interest, and when Kathy opened her paper at breakfast the next morning, Freda Cowley's face was staring up at her. Above it, heavy black newsprint demanded, 'Do you know this woman?'

Kathy dropped the paper, her hands flying to her mouth. '*Guy! Guy!* Come quickly!'

He husband dashed downstairs, swung round the newel-post and hurried into the kitchen. 'What is it? What's happened? You sounded—' He broke off, staring down at the paper on the table. 'Dead? Oh my God!'

Kathy said tremblingly, 'No wonder she disappeared without telling anyone. And when I think what I said about her!'

Guy put an arm round her and bent to read the newsprint. 'Found in a ditch yesterday—dead about ten days. That's just when she disappeared, isn't it, ten days ago?' He could feel his wife shaking, and his arm tightened. 'Sit down, love, and have a drink of coffee. I'll pour it for you.'

'They don't know who she is. We'll have to phone and tell them.'

'Probably half Westridge has been on by now.'

'All the same, we'll have to.'

Guy hesitated. 'I suppose we are sure it's Freda? I mean—'

'Of course we are. They describe her dress, too.' Kathy's eyes filled. 'Guy, I was with her when she bought it, at Faversham's.'

'All right, all right. Who do I have to ring?'

'It's a Shillingham number.'

She held her coffee-cup with both hands, taking tiny sips of the scalding liquid and trying to stop herself from shaking. Out in the hall, she could hear her husband dialling, then his voice with a slight tremor in it.

'I'm ringing about the sketch in this morning's paper. We think we know who the woman is. Her name is Mrs Freda Cowley, of Hinckley's Cottage, Westridge.'

CHAPTER 6

The man looked shaken, Webb reflected, but that was only natural. His wife, too. Striking-looking woman, with those unusual eyes.

'So you'd no personal dealings with Mrs Cowley, sir?'

'None whatever. I dealt with the agents, Bayliss of Marlton.'

'You say you were up the previous week. You didn't meet her then?'

'No, the cottage wasn't available at the time. The agent phoned a couple of days later.'

'And you took it sight unseen? That was quite a risk, wasn't it, when it's to be your home for a month? Even more so, since your wife has special requirements at the moment.'

'I checked there was a downstairs lavatory. That was our only "special requirement".'

'But wouldn't it have been wiser to see it for yourself before deciding?'

'Chief Inspector, I wanted to be in Westridge, it hadn't looked as though I was going to manage it, then this suddenly came up. Why look a gift horse in the mouth? And since we're perfectly satisfied with the place, I can't see that any of this is relevant.'

'The agents said they'd received instructions from the owner?'

'That's right.' Selby paused. 'She must have posted them just before she was killed.'

'But suppose,' Webb said heavily, his eyes on the man's face, 'she hadn't intended going away?'

'I don't think she did,' Jessica interrupted jerkily. 'She didn't tell her cleaner, and that woman who phoned insisted she was expected.'

'What woman was that, ma'am?'

The conversation with Wilma Bernstein was repeated.

'But if she hadn't intended going away,' Jessica said, 'who sent the agent the keys?'

'My God!' Matthew's face whitened. Webb had wondered how long it would take them to question that. 'You mean her killer posted them?'

'Clever, really. While people might wonder at an empty house, if a tenancy'd been arranged, no one would worry.'

Jessica frowned. 'But the bed linen and towels were clean. She must . . . I mean, unless . . . Oh God!'

Which was a point he hadn't reached himself, Webb reflected. They had a cold-blooded customer on their hands this time. 'When you arrived, ma'am, there was nothing to make you suspect all was not as it should be?'

'No, nothing. I did wonder at her leaving valuable china on the shelves, but only fleetingly.'

'There were no personal belongings about, which you'd expect her to have taken with her?'

They both shook their heads. Which explained the suitcase in the burnt-out car. That the victim proved to be its missing owner had come as no surprise.

'Have there been any other phone calls for Mrs Cowley since you arrived?'

Jessica hesitated. 'One, yes. From someone called Charles.'

'You don't know his surname?'

She said unwillingly, 'Actually, we met him later. Charles Palmer. He didn't want it mentioned in front of his wife.'

'We'll be as tactful as we can. Now I'm afraid I'll have to ask you to vacate the house for a few hours. Scenes of Crime officers are on their way.'

'You don't think she was killed *here*?' Jessica's voice rose.

'It's possible, ma'am, but that's not all they'll be looking for.'

'But where are we to go?' Matthew demanded. 'You can't just—'

'Well, sir, since it's almost lunch-time, I suggest you have a leisurely meal and then perhaps go for a drive.'

'Now look,' Matthew began truculently, 'is this really necessary? We've been here a week ourselves; surely we'll have obliterated anything of use?'

'There'll still be traces, sir. Fingerprints, an odd hair. It's amazing what these chaps come up with. If you'll collect your handbag, ma'am, and anything else you need, we can leave together and I'll take the keys.'

'They didn't accept with very good grace,' Webb remarked to Jackson as they got into their car. 'Can't say I blame them, but murder's seldom convenient.'

'You know who she is, don't you, Guv?'

'Who who is?'

'Mrs Selby. She's Jessica Randal, the actress. I recognized her. Millie has a magazine with their photographs in. They've not been married long.'

'You're a fund of information, Ken.'

'Millie'd like her autograph, I bet.'

'Well, I'm damned if I'm going to get it for her. Now for the cleaner. I didn't want to interview her at the Markhams', but she should be back by now.'

Jackson nodded. The Governor always liked to see people in their own homes. 'She lives in Donkey Lane, the steep road we came down from the top.'

Carrie Speight opened the door immediately. Her face was white and her eyes red-rimmed from weeping.

'I'm sorry to disturb you,' Webb said gently, 'but I'm afraid there are some questions we must ask you.'

She nodded and stepped to one side. 'You'd better come in.'

Webb ducked his head as he went through the low doorway into the cottage. Though smaller and less opulent than Hinckley's, it was neat, clean and cheerful. At her uncertain gesture of invitation, the two policemen seated themselves on the chintz chairs.

'Now, Miss Speight, how long had you worked for Mrs Cowley?'

Tears brimmed again and Carrie bit her lip. 'Must be three years now. Such a kind lady, she was. She used to give me her blouses and things, when she got tired of them. Some of them had hardly been worn. Of course they needed altering, but I'm quite good with my needle.' She broke off, ended in a whisper, 'I'm sorry, sir. I shouldn't run on like that.'

'That's all right, miss. You live with your sister, Mrs Markham was saying.'

'Yes, sir. She works at the hairdresser's.'

'Here in Westridge?'

'Yes, and they're glad to have her. She could get a job in Shillingham any day, but she doesn't fancy the journey.'

Webb guessed the bus service would be infrequent, and about a forty-minute ride each way. 'Will she have heard yet, about Mrs Cowley?'

'I don't know, sir. We don't get a paper, but someone at the salon might have told her.'

'She wouldn't have known her as well as you did?'

'Well, she did her hair, like. A lot of the ladies go to Della. She's very good.'

'When was the last time you saw Mrs Cowley?'

Carrie wiped her eyes on the corner of her apron, a gesture that struck Jackson as medieval. 'Tuesday it was, sir, week before last. My tooth had been bad, but I went to Hinckley's as usual. I don't like letting people down. But Mrs Cowley saw I was in pain, and she phoned her own dentist in Shillingham. Made an emergency appointment and drove me there herself. Then she waited while they did the filling, and brought me home again. She even came in with me, to make sure I'd got aspirins for the pain. I never dreamed I wouldn't see her again.'

Carrie broke down and sobbed for several minutes, while Webb pulled at his lip reflectively.

'Could I have the name and address of the dentist, miss?' He'd provide the definitive ID if no relatives came forward.

'Mr Carruthers, in Kimberly Road. Number twenty-four, I think.'

A successful one, then. Kimberly Road was Shillingham's Harley Street. 'Now, miss, had Mrs Cowley any relatives that you know of?'

'Only her husband, like.'

'You knew him?'

'Oh yes, sir. Leastways, I only saw him a couple of times,

when he was home with the 'flu. He was usually at work when I was there, and then of course he moved away.'

'Any idea where he is now?'

'No, sir.' Carrie looked up suddenly. 'You don't think *he*—?'

'We don't think anything at the moment, miss. Now, who was she friendly with, in the village?'

'I don't really know. Mrs Markham, I suppose, but they weren't that close.' She coloured. 'Mrs Cowley preferred gentlemen's company.'

'And who were they? You won't be breaking any confidences, Miss Speight. It can only help Mrs Cowley now.'

'Well, sir, I did take one or two phone calls for her. There was Mr Palmer and someone called Richard. They never gave their names, but Mrs Cowley sometimes mentioned them. Oh, and Major Hartley. I recognized his voice.'

'Were they regular callers?'

'Mr Palmer was, at least once a week. And there was another gentleman who phoned a lot. I don't know his name, but I don't think he was from the village.'

'Did you meet any of them?'

'I know Mr Palmer by sight, sir, but I never saw any of them at Hinckley's.' She paused, then added loyally, 'Mrs Cowley was very lonely, sir.'

'And the gentlemen's wives didn't understand them.'

'Probably not,' Carrie agreed earnestly. 'Ever so kind, Mrs Cowley, if anyone was in trouble.'

Webb felt it best to change the subject. 'When the Selbys engaged you, did you notice anything different about the cottage?'

'Only their things, like.'

'Nothing unaccountably out of place—anything like that?'

'I did wonder where the washing was. Mrs Cowley changes the bed on Fridays and puts the sheets in the basket and I wash them as soon as I get there. But when—I mean, that Friday there was no answer when I rang the bell, though she hadn't told me she'd be away. So when I went back on Tuesday, and Mrs Selby asked me to stay, I looked in the laundry basket, but it was empty. I thought perhaps Mrs Cowley'd sent them to the laundry, so as not to leave dirty things for people coming to the house.'

In which case, Webb reflected grimly, Mrs Selby had probably been right and the killer had changed the bed-clothes, ready for the tenants he hoped would take the cottage. Very likely the woman had actually been killed in the bed, by someone she regarded as a 'lover'.

He said, 'Didn't I see you in the distance last week, at The Willows?'

'That's right, sir. I work there on Wednesdays.'

'It's been a bad month for the village, hasn't it?'

She bit her lip and nodded.

'Only comfort is, we've more to go on, now.'

Her head jerked back, eyes flying to his face. 'But you don't think it's the same man?'

Webb was surprised. Would she prefer both a rapist and a murderer at large? 'It's more than likely.' Yet Stapleton had been unable to establish rape and there were no signs of knife pricks on the body.

'But if he'd already killed once, surely he'd have killed Sister?'

She had a point there, but the common link of both the village of Westridge and the jingles was too strong to overlook. And at the time the rapist was demanding nursery rhymes of Fran Daly, only the murderer knew the dead woman had one in her pocket.

'Well, don't worry about it, Miss Speight. We'll soon catch him.' He stood up, nodding to Jackson. 'There are three pubs in the village, I believe. What are they like?'

'The Orange Tree's the smartest, sir, and the only one with a restaurant, though you can get bar snacks at the others.'

'OK, Ken,' Webb said, strapping himself into the car, 'back to the cottage. The SOCOs should be there any

minute. Then we'll go and have a bite to eat at The Orange
Tree. It's the nearest pub to Hinckley's, and good landlords
know quite a bit of what's going on. We can kill two birds
with one stone.'

In the restaurant at The Orange Tree, Jessica was toying
with her glass. 'I felt a bit mean, dropping Charles Palmer
in the soup.'

'You had little option, my love. It's never wise to withold
evidence.'

'Oh, but surely—' She broke off and her eyes widened.
'You don't mean he might have done it?'

'Of course he might have done it. At this stage, anyone
might.'

'But he knows I know his connection with Freda. Suppose
he tries to shut me up?'

'He'll be too late, won't he?' Matthew rejoined calmly.
'And come to think of it, if he had killed her, he'd hardly
ring up, would he, let alone identify himself.'

'A double bluff, perhaps. Or he could have been checking
that the cottage had been let.'

Matthew gave a short laugh. 'I know you sometimes *act*
in murder plays, darling, but you should try your hand at
writing them!'

'He could have been at the Markhams', though. The
murderer, I mean.'

'True.'

'And I thought I was going to be bored in the country!
Only here a week, and we've had rape and murder, not to
mention our house being turned over by the police.'

'It's a bloody nuisance. I was getting on so well this
morning.'

'All the same, darling, once you knew your landlady'd
been done away with, even your concentration might have
been broken.'

He held her artless gaze for a moment, then laughed
shamefacedly. 'We're a selfish lot, we writers. Of course I'm

sorry for the poor woman, but it is damned inconvenient. Still, since our home is barred for the next few hours, what would you like to do?'

On the other side of the panelled wall, Webb and Jackson had settled with their pints and, having identified themselves, invited the landlord to join them. Jeff Soames was a tall man, with thin strands of hair laid hopefully across his balding pate. He had shoulders like a Rugby forward.

'A shock about Mrs Cowley,' he said gloomily. 'I suppose that's why you're here?'

'That's right. You knew her, of course?'

'Oh yes, and her old man, before he upped and left her.'

The Markhams had mentioned that. 'Has she been in recently?'

'Yes, she was quite a regular.' He paused. 'Popular, too.'

'Especially with the gentlemen?'

'You've heard, have you?' Soames seemed relieved. 'Well, she went a bit wild, like, after he'd gone. Nice woman, though. I was sorry for her—and not the only one. She'd plenty of willing comforters, from all I hear.'

'Any names, Mr Soames?'

The landlord looked alarmed. 'Oh, now look, sir, hold hard! They're my regulars too, some of 'em. My bread and butter, as you might say. How'd they feel about me shopping them to the police?'

'One of them might have killed her.'

The man swallowed. 'Yes—well. As long as you keep it confidential, like.' Some half-dozen names followed, among them a couple Carrie Speight had mentioned. Jackson noted them down.

'When was the last time you saw Mrs Cowley?'

'The Wednesday, it must have been. Almost two weeks ago. She was in at lunch-time, bright as a button, chatting to that gentleman.' He jerked his head in the direction of the dining-room.

Webb straightened, his eyes narrowing. 'What gentleman is that, sir?'

'Why, the one that's taken her cottage. Mr Selby, isn't it? When I heard he'd moved in, I reckoned they must have fixed it over lunch. They left together, and all.'

'You're quite sure it was Mr Selby she was with?'

'Well, she didn't come in with him, like. He was here first. He chatted to me at the bar for a while, asked if there were any cottages to rent around here. Then he took his steak and kidney to that table over there, and soon after Mrs Cowley came in. She bought her usual lager and took it across to his table. I heard her say something like, 'All alone, are you? So am I!'

'Then what happened?'

'Well, sir, the bar filled up and I was kept fairly busy. I didn't notice much else. Mr Selby bought himself another drink, and one for her too, and a bit later I saw them leave together.'

'And that was Wednesday lunch-time, the fifth of September?'

'Reckon that was the date, yes.'

Webb felt a tingle of excitement. That might well have been the last time she was seen alive—and in the company of Matthew Selby, who'd denied all knowledge of her. He said casually, 'Is there another way out of the dining-room?'

'No, sir, they have to come through here.'

'And have you by any chance somewhere we could talk privately?'

'There's the parlour, sir. First door on the left along the passage.'

'Fine. Thanks very much, Mr Soames. Now, I think we'll sample some of that steak and kidney you mentioned.'

The man nodded and thankfully moved away. Jackson gave a low whistle. 'And what do you make of that, Guv?'

'Interesting, Ken. Very interesting. What exactly did Selby say about her—can you check?'

Jackson thumbed through his notebook. 'First off, he said

he'd had no personal dealings with her. Then when you asked if they'd met when he was up before, he said, "No, the cottage wasn't available at the time."' Jackson looked up, his blue eyes brilliant with excitement. 'Looks as though he took steps to make it available, doesn't it?'

'We mustn't jump the gun, Ken, but the man has to be crazy. Surely he knew we'd check? Well, we'll have another word with Mr Matthew Selby as soon as he's had his lunch.'

To Jackson's relief, they'd finished eating themselves before the Selbys emerged from the restaurant. Webb eased himself out of his chair and moved slowly across to intercept them. Selby looked surprised, but not worried, to see him.

'I'd like another word, sir, if you can spare us a moment. No need to trouble your wife. Perhaps she'd care to wait for you here.'

'If you're sure this is really necessary.'

'Oh, I am, sir.'

Selby glanced at him quickly, then helped his wife to a corner table, propping her crutches against the wall. Webb saw the quick, anxious glance she sent him. In silence the three men walked to the small parlour. Webb ushered Selby ahead of him, and Jackson closed the door behind them.

'I really don't see the point of this, Chief Inspector. It's barely two hours since we spoke to you, and you covered everything pretty exhaustively then.'

'We now believe, sir, that the statement you made was incorrect.'

He frowned. 'In what way?'

'You stated, sir, twice, that you'd never met Mrs Freda Cowley.'

'So?'

'You still maintain that, sir?'

'Of course I do.'

'The landlord here informs us that you lunched together on the fifth of September.'

Selby stared at him for several minutes. Webb could

have sworn his expression was total incomprehension. Then
either understanding or memory filtered through, and with
it a dawning horror. And Jackson had said it was his wife
who did the acting.

'*That* was Freda Cowley? I swear to God I'd no idea!'

'Perhaps,' said Webb pleasantly, 'you'd like to start again,
sir. Had you arranged to meet Mrs Cowley here?'

'For God's sake, man! I'd never seen her before in my
life. She just brought her drink to my table, that's all.'

'You sat talking for some time and left together.'

Selby moistened his lips. 'But we didn't exchange names.
You don't, in those circumstances. It was just a casual
conversation between strangers.'

'What did you talk about, sir?'

'I told her I was hoping to rent a cottage here. She said
she hadn't heard of anywhere available. Then we talked
quite a lot about America. I said I was going over later in
the year, and she'd stayed with friends out there.'

'You left with her.'

'We went out of the door together, yes. I offered her a lift,
but she said she only lived round the corner, so I left her
and drove back to the Hall. I never thought about her
again.'

'That would be Sandon Hall, sir? What time did you
arrive there?'

'God, I don't know. About two-thirty.'

There was a silence. Webb was idly tracing the cracks on
the table with his fingernail. 'As you know, sir, I was always
bothered about you taking the cottage unseen. That's why
I asked several times if you'd met Mrs Cowley. Now it turns
out you had. And since you left here at the same time, what
more natural than her inviting you back, for coffee, perhaps?'

'That's bloody ridiculous! I didn't *know* the woman, it
was just a chance encounter.'

'But we're told, sir, that Mrs Cowley was a lady who
made the most of such encounters. And, if you'll forgive me,
your wife's out of bounds, so to speak, and I believe you've

not been married long. Tough luck that is, sir.'

A dull red flush suffused Selby's face. He started out of his chair, and sank slowly back again. 'By God,' he said thickly, 'if you weren't a police officer, I'd give you a bloody nose for that!'

'*Did* Mrs Cowley invite you back with her, sir?'

'No, she did not.'

'Did you suggest it yourself?'

'Definitely and categorically not.'

'You see, sir,' Webb said softly, 'from what we've established so far, it's just possible that you were the last person to see her alive. Apart from her murderer, that is.'

Selby sank his head into his hands. Jackson saw they were trembling. When he raised it again, his face was haggard.

He said, 'I can see it looks bad, my denying having met her. *But I didn't know I had!* I'd even forgotten sitting with a woman over lunch, though of course I remember now. My mind was full of other things—the meeting with the Sandons, finding accommodation, getting back to my wife in London. But I swear to God our conversation was entirely innocent. My wife could have overheard every word of it.'

'It didn't occur to you, when the agents phoned, that the cottage belonged to the woman you'd lunched with?'

'Why the hell should it? And let's get things straight. I didn't *lunch* with her. You make it sound like an assignation. I was eating my lunch, and she came and sat at my table. That's all there was to it.'

'Convenient, though, wasn't it, the cottage coming on the market just as you needed it.'

'I wasn't desperate enough to murder for it, if that's what you're getting at.'

'So you reckon it was about two-fifteen when the pair of you left here?'

'About that.'

'And your car was parked—where?'

'Round the back, in the car park.'

'Did you see which direction she took?'

'She turned right.'

'As though she was going home?'

'Yes, though I didn't know that.'

'Did anyone else leave at the same time?'

'I think there were a couple of men behind us. I didn't pay much attention.'

'So when you last saw Mrs Cowley, she was alone and walking back towards her cottage?'

'Yes.' Selby hesitated. 'How do you know no one else saw her?'

'Someone might have, sir, but if so, they haven't come forward yet. Mrs Markham rang her at nine the next morning, Thursday, and there was no reply. Since the agents phoned you on the Friday, they must have received the keys in the post that morning. It seems probable she was killed the day you saw her.'

Selby asked in a low voice, '*How* was she killed?'

'Suffocation, after a blow to the head knocked her unconscious.'

'Poor soul,' he said softly.

'And there's nothing else you can tell us, sir? She didn't say what she was doing that afternoon?'

'No.'

'Very well, that's all for the moment.'

Webb made no attempt to rise. Selby blundered to his feet and Jackson opened the door for him. Jessica was waiting anxiously in the saloon bar, oblivious of the approving glances coming her way. As Matthew reached her, she blurted out, 'What is it? What's happened?'

'Let's get out of here.' Matthew was aware of the landlord's eyes following them as they left the room. Last time he'd come to the bloody Orange Tree.

'Darling, what *is* it?'

He paused in the act of opening the car door, leaning briefly on its roof. 'I suspect they think I'm the murderer.'

'*What?*'

'I had met her, Jessica. How about that? She chatted me

up while I was lunching here. But I swear before God I didn't know who she was.'

'My darling, I believe you!'

'Get in the car. I'll tell you as we drive along. I need to get away from this bloody village for a while.' He tossed her crutches on to the back seat and helped her into the front. She was suddenly frightened. They couldn't really suspect Matthew, surely? But he hadn't mentioned meeting this woman, name or no name. Why? Because he hadn't thought it important? Or because it was too important?

They drove rapidly past their cottage. Several cars were drawn up outside, and the front door stood open. The Scenes of Crime people, the Chief Inspector called them. Did that mean their house was the scene of crime? She shuddered, imagining them poking and prying among her things, perhaps finding evidence of murder. She said suddenly, 'This hasn't changed your mind about staying here, has it? You don't want to go back to London?'

'That would start them talking, wouldn't it?' He shook his head grimly. 'I'm sorry, darling, we'll have to stick it out. I'm not going to be driven away by a nosey landlord and a policeman who's too big for his boots. God, some of the things he hinted at!'

'What kind of things?'

'Unrepeatable. I'd like to sue him.'

She laid a hand over his. 'Darling, don't take it too personally. They're probably like that with everyone.'

'Not everyone has drinks with a murder victim just before she cops it.'

'She was killed that day?'

'They seem to think so.'

'Do they know at what time?'

'I doubt it, after ten days.'

Jessica shivered. 'Anyway you went back to the Hall after lunch.'

'Yes, but I didn't see anyone. Dom had gone off shooting, he told me to let myself in. I just went to the library and worked by myself for a couple of hours. There were servants about, but I didn't see any and I don't suppose they saw me. Not much of an alibi. I left about four and drove home.'

As they reached the main road and turned in the direction of Heatherton, Matthew relaxed slightly. He glanced at his wife's taut face and patted her hand. 'Never mind, my love, at least it has publicity value. "Biographer in murder inquiry." Quite a ring to it, hasn't it?'

CHAPTER 7

James Bayliss stared at the policeman the other side of his desk. 'You're telling me these instructions *didn't* come from the owner of the cottage?'

He spoke, Jackson thought, like an Army officer addressing the ranks. Even looked like one, with his greying hair and small military moustache.

'It would seem not, sir. On the day this was dated, Mrs Cowley had been asked about accommodation in the village. If she'd been going to let herself, she'd surely have said.' Webb glanced at the letter. 'Is it a good copy of her signature, would you say?'

'I've no idea. I'd never heard of the lady till that arrived.'

'You haven't still got the envelope, I suppose?'

'No, I haven't, Chief Inspector. It came more than a week ago. In any case, I can't see what use it would have been.'

'We might have established the blood group, sir, from saliva traces on the stamp. The characteristics are often present in other body fluids.' Even a negative result would have helped, Webb thought morosely. For had the substances *not* been present, showing the sender to be one of the unhelpful fourteen per cent who didn't secrete them— then he was almost certainly Nurse Daly's attacker as well.

Bayliss accepted the information without comment. He placed the tips of his fingers together, making a pyramid, and regarded them sternly over its apex. 'Am I permitted to know, then, who *did* send that letter?'

'Very likely the murderer, sir. It seems he planned carefully. Left the cottage ready for tenants to move in.'

The man's lips tightened. 'I must say I resent being duped in this way. I'd no reason whatever—'

'Of course not.' Webb paused. 'Now, sir, about Mr Selby. You checked the contents with him, I suppose?'

'My son did.' He still spoke crisply. The family firm was eighty years old, and nothing remotely shady had touched it before. Now, through no fault of his own, it would be linked in the public's mind with murder. It really wasn't good enough.

'So you've not seen the property yourself?'

Bayliss forced his mind back to the issue at hand. 'Oh yes. I drove over when the keys arrived, to see if it was suitable for Mr Selby.'

'That would be Friday morning. Did you notice anything unusual about the place?'

'Only that the milk and papers hadn't been cancelled. There were two pints on the step, and two *Daily Mails*, one on the hall floor and one in the letter-box. I called at the post office, and the woman said she'd speak to the milkman. No point in advertising that the place was empty.'

'Did she seem surprised Mrs Cowley hadn't notified her?'

'Quite the contrary. She laughed and said something like, "That's Mrs Cowley all over."'

Had the killer banked on that reaction? Webb wondered. If so, it implied he knew his victim. But he could hardly have cancelled them himself.

'Is it unusual, sir, to receive keys through the post like that?'

'Unusual, yes, but it didn't strike us as sinister.'

'If we could have a word with your son, then.'

Though Webb had met Julian Bayliss before, neither betrayed the fact and the older man noticed nothing. Nor had the boy anything useful to impart. Taking the typewrit-

ten letter with them, Webb and Jackson returned to Shillingham. There'd been a typewriter at the cottage. Ten to one,
it would prove to be the one used. And for the rhyme in the
dead woman's pocket.

His phone was ringing as Webb reached his office and he
stretched across the desk to answer it. Pips bleeped briefly
in his ear, followed by the sound of a coin falling. Then a
woman's tentative voice: 'Chief Inspector Webb?'

'Speaking.' He hitched himself on to the corner of the
desk.

'Good afternoon. I saw your advertisement in the paper.'

The anonymous letter-writer! Webb caught Crombie's
curious eye and gave him a thumbs-up. 'Yes, madam. Thank
you for phoning. Is it possible for us to meet?'

'I'm afraid not.' It wasn't a young voice, and Webb
guessed the stress even this call was causing her. 'In any
case, I can't think it would help. But I'll try to answer your
questions.'

'Thank you. First, then, exactly when and where did this
incident take place?'

'Three years ago last June, in Ashmartin Park.'

He said gently, 'Could you tell me what happened?'

'I was on my way home from Mothers' Union. It was
about nine-thirty, but still quite light. I remember wondering what time they locked the park for the night. He—he
stepped out of some bushes just behind me, and put a knife
to the back of my neck.' Webb closed his eyes briefly as his
last, wild hope that this could be a different attacker faded
away. 'Then he pulled a woollen helmet over my head.
Some kind of Balaclava, I think, but back to front so that I
couldn't see anything. And he—dragged me back into the
bushes.'

As her voice faltered, a rapid bleeping sounded in his ear,
indicating that the money was used up. Webb swore softly,
praying she wouldn't let the connection go. To his relief,
another coin rattled home.

'You mentioned nursery rhymes,' he prompted.

'That's right. He wouldn't allow me to stop. They seemed to—to goad him, somehow.' Her voice warmed with anger. 'Can you imagine, Mr Webb, what I go through, when my grandchildren request them now? It's ruined their babyhood for me.'

'There's no way you'd recognize this man, if you saw him?'

'None at all. He tied my hands, and I could scarcely breathe in the helmet, let alone see anything.'

'His voice?'

'A whisper only. I'd no idea it could sound so sinister.'

'You haven't heard reports of similar incidents?'

'Not until now. I'm not surprised, though. Not many women would come forward, after an experience like that.'

Webb sighed and stood up. 'I'm sorry to have distressed you by going through it again, but I assure you it was most helpful. Thank you very much for contacting me.' He put the phone down and looked at it thoughtfully. 'By tomorrow, the papers will have connected the murder with the rape. Thank God I spoke to her before she realized she'd been with a murderer. Right, Alan.' He straightened, and his voice became brisker. 'Arrange a briefing, will you, in an hour's time. The first priority is blood tests for all males in and near the village, if we can twist their arms sufficiently. Given the secretion factor, that could rule out ninety-nine per cent of them. At the same time, check if any of them has any connection with Ashmartin. You can make a start on the names Carrie Speight gave us. No word on the ex-husband yet?'

'Nothing's come through here.'

Webb sat down at his desk. 'I had another session with PC Frost, but he can't come up with a motive other than possible blackmail.'

'Was there anyone who'd a lot to lose if his association with her got out?'

'That, my lad, is what we'll have to discover.'

His phone rang again. It was the editor of the *Broadshire News*. 'Hi, Dave. This murder business. Any crumbs you can drop an old pal before the big boys scoop the lot?'

Webb smiled. 'Don't say I never do anything for you! Two things, both of which will be public property tomorrow. One: the murdered woman had a typed nursery rhyme in her pocket.' He heard Romilly's low whistle. 'And two, the couple who've taken her cottage are apparently celebrities, Matthew Selby and Jessica Randal. No doubt their names mean more to you than they did to me.'

'Bless you, Dave! We'll pull out all the stops. Cheers.'

At his desk across the town, Michael Romilly reached for the internal phone. This was front page stuff all right. Just occasionally it paid, being local.

'Jill? My office, please, at the double.' He dropped the receiver and frowned momentarily, resenting the forced note in his voice. He was still uneasy in her presence, and the fact annoyed him. A year ago, when his marriage was going through a bad patch, they'd had a brief affair, though he acknowledged it had been more than that to Jill. Pity, she was a nice girl. When it ended and Kate came back, he'd expected her to hand in her notice. She hadn't, and he could scarcely ask her to go. In any case, she was a damn good reporter.

He looked up as, after a brief tap on the door, she came in.

'Yes, boss?' She hadn't used his name since they broke up.

'This murder the nationals have got their teeth into.' He kept his gaze on the paper on his desk, preferring to meet the dead woman's eyes rather than Jill's. 'Seems to be linked with the nursery rhyme rape in Westridge. What's more, the victim's cottage has been taken by the biographer Matthew Selby, who won some literary prize a year or two ago, and his actress wife Jessica Randal. I want this in tonight's edition, so high-tail it out there, will you, and phone in a report? The photos will have to wait till tomorrow, unless we can dig some out of the library.'

Jill hesitated. 'I won't be treading on Bill's toes?'

Another cause for embarrassment. They both knew she was wasting her time on the Woman's Page; she was as capable as Bill Hardy of being chief reporter. Michael hadn't admitted, even to himself, that by restricting her scope, he hoped to needle her into leaving.

'You want the woman's angle, I suppose,' she added, her voice without inflection.

'You'll make the front page with this—what more do you want? But only if you get a move on—we're pushing it as it is.'

Jill's calm brown eyes rested briefly on his bent head. Then she nodded and left the room. Fool! she chided herself, as she got quickly into her Mini and fastened the seat-belt. You won't get any change out of him, so don't expect it. And no promotion, either, she reflected, threading her way through the traffic with practised ease. She was ambitious, but for the moment she was tied to Broadshire. Her married sister had been paralysed in a road accident and Jill, pleased to be needed, had moved in with her indefinitely, to run the house and feed the family. Fleet Street would have to wait, but she'd get there one day, and by her own efforts, with no thanks to Michael Romilly.

The familiar pain rose in her and she fought it down. It was over. Had been for almost a year. The fact that she still loved him was her bad luck, and she'd have to live with it.

With an effort, she changed her line of thought. She'd never been to Westridge. It wasn't a village you passed through on the way to anywhere else. Turning off the Heatherton road, she pushed her personal problems aside and concentrated on the task ahead.

'I told you there was publicity value in this!' Matthew shut the door behind the last reporter. 'That girl yesterday opened the floodgates.'

Jessica leant back against the sofa and closed her eyes. 'I've a feeling they're more interested in the house than in us, since it might be the scene of the crime.'

'The police took the typewriter, by the way. Lucky I brought my own after all.'

'That was the one which—?'

'No doubt that's what they're ascertaining. Carrie's a bit subdued this morning, isn't she?'

'I'm subdued myself,' Jessica retorted with a touch of asperity. 'And don't forget she was fond of Mrs Cowley. It must be a terrible shock.' She looked up at him. 'What was she like?'

'Attractive, in a rather brittle way. Suspiciously blonde hair, well made up but rather a lot of it. Talked quickly, in short sentences.'

'It's hard to reconcile the *femme fatale* image with Carrie's sainted benefactor. Did it occur to you she might be? A siren, I mean?'

'Not really. She wasn't that obvious. I shouldn't think she hired herself out, for instance. But free with her favours —yes, I can accept that.' He studied his wife's pensive face. 'But she did *not* offer them to me, and for my part, nothing was further from my mind. Does that answer your unspoken question?'

She smiled and flushed. 'Sorry, darling. I wasn't really thinking that.'

'If you weren't, you must be the only one.'

'What do you mean?'

'Our friend the Chief Inspector reckons I'm a good candidate.' He turned away, feeling for his cigarettes. 'Well, that's enough disruption for one day. I must get down to work. See you at lunch.'

Jessica nodded and picked up the *Daily Telegraph*. It, too, reported on the murder. Tomorrow, no doubt, it would carry the interview they'd just given.

The doorbell again. She looked helplessly about for her crutches, but Carrie came running down the stairs and, with a strained smile at her, went to open it. Leo Sandon stood on the step.

'Good day, good day!' he boomed. 'Is the lady of the house at home?'

The lady of the house, thought Jessica, was lying on a mortuary slab somewhere. But she called out, 'I'm here, Leo. Please come in.'

He bent his head to go through the doorway, his luminous dark eyes on hers. He was wearing a purple shirt, black cord jeans and open sandals, and a leather shoulder-bag of the type affected by continental males hung from his shoulder. His toes, Jessica noted in one all-embracing glance, were as long and thin as the rest of him.

'Madame!' He took her hand and raised it to his lips. Over his stooping shoulder, Jessica saw Carrie's pale surprise.

She said weakly, 'I thought you were another reporter.'

He smiled benignly down on her, restored to his full height. 'You've entertained the gentlemen of the press? How diligent of them, to sniff you out so soon.'

'It was only because of the murder—'

'Murder?' he interrupted, frowning. 'What murder?'

Jessica stared at him. It had filled her mind to the exclusion of all else for the last twenty-four hours, and she found it impossible to accept that there was anyone, at least locally, who hadn't heard of it.

'Mrs Cowley's murder. The lady whose house this is.'

'But how unfortunate,' he said, as if a cricket match had been rained off. 'Poor woman. Still, it hardly concerns you, does it?'

'There are those,' Jessica said drily, 'who might not agree with you.'

'Really? You surprise me.' He paused. 'You haven't forgotten your little promise, I hope?'

She made an effort to meet him on his own terms. At least it would offer temporary distraction. 'To read your poems? Of course not. I've—been looking forward to it.'

His face lit up. 'Splendid—so have I.'

Above their heads, the wail of a vacuum cleaner started up, and he frowned. Jessica said quickly, 'We could go in the garden if you like, but I'll have to ask for your assistance.'

'My dear lady! With the greatest pleasure!'

He reminded her, Jessica thought, fighting down hysterical laughter, of one of the great actors of the past. Beerbohm Tree, perhaps, or Henry Irving. His voice was resonant and beautifully cultured. It was just that he seemed a century out of date.

They processed—there was no other word for it—through to the kitchen and thence out of the back door. Carrie had put two deckchairs on the lawn earlier, in case Jessica wanted to go outside. The morning was warm and overcast, a world of green and grey. Leo settled her, with a great deal of fussing, in one of the chairs, and pulled the other round to face her before seating himself. With his long legs almost under his chin, he looked like a praying mantis.

'Now,' he said, his voice vibrant with excitement, 'for the recitation!' From the leather shoulder-bag he produced a slim, beautifully bound volume, and Jessica exclaimed in surprise.

'So you *have* been published! Matthew thought—'

But he shook his head. 'No, no. A conceit only, printed at my own expense. May I suggest you commence with *The Wild Wind*. I lay awake last night, and seemed to hear your voice speaking the words.'

He leafed through the pages, found what he was looking for, and, bending forward, passed the book to Jessica. Its pages were heavy vellum and in the centre of the opened one were six lines of uneven length. Diffidently she flicked it over, but a new title was displayed on the next one.

'It's just this page?'

He smiled. 'No doubt you'd heard I write long verses. That's true. The majority are two or three pages, but this one was a particularly happy creation—a small gem, as I hope you'll agree. I was able to say all I wanted in half a dozen lines. Now, will you read it, please?'

Jessica had rapidly scanned the lines, none of which boasted a capital letter or any punctuation. Hoping fervently that she was putting in the expression he desired, she proclaimed as awesomely as its brevity allowed:

'o formless being
whose passing bends the trees
who whispers to me in the still of night tho never seen
take at the last my breath
that never dying
I may roam eternal night with thee'

As she finished there was a brief pause. Leo was gazing at her raptly, his hands clasped together. At last he gave a deep sigh. 'I *knew* it!' he breathed. 'I knew it would touch you, as it does me. Thank you, thank you.'

Feeling she'd hardly earned such praise, Jessica said tentatively, 'Shall I read another?' and immediately regretted her offer. For the next poem he selected was indeed long, and at first glance she hadn't the remotest idea what it was about. Thankful for her practice in reading unseen prose, she ploughed into it, occasional swift glances reassuring her that her rendition was meeting with Leo's approval. He seemed to have selected in this poem all his favourite words and strung them haphazardly together, so that, provided you didn't try to make sense of it, it sounded beautiful. She hoped she'd remember enough to regale Matthew with over lunch. And surely it was lunch-time now? She daren't risk a glance at her watch—it would be too pointed. Matthew —Carrie! Come to my rescue, please!

But when, some fifteen minutes later, the interruption came, it was not what she expected. She was floundering through yet another obscure verse when her voice was suddenly drowned by the approach of a low-flying helicopter. Thankfully, she broke off, but the effect on Leo was astounding. He leapt to his feet, overturning the deckchair in the process, his face contorted with fury.

'Be off with you!' he screamed, shaking his fists at the hovering machine. 'Don't imagine you can frighten me!'

The pilot, assuming Leo was trying to attract his attention, came lower still, making lazy arcs over the garden as he attempted to discover what all the fuss was about.

'Spies! Filthy spies!' Leo was ranting. 'Mayn't we even read poetry in a garden now, without attracting notice? Get away—do you hear me? Be gone this minute!' Beside himself with rage, he turned, caught up the deckchair, and smashed it back on the ground. Above the noise of his shouting and the throbbing of the aircraft, Jessica heard a crack. She had never seen anyone literally dance with rage and she watched, mesmerized, until, bored with the performance, the helicopter moved away. Leo promptly burst into tears. For some sixty seconds he sobbed with complete abandon, tears gushing unchecked from his eyes. Then he stopped as suddenly as he'd begun, took a handkerchief from his pocket and blew his nose. He smiled at Jessica, entirely without embarrassment.

'It'll go on my report,' he said in his normal voice. 'One more black mark against me. I'm aware that my room is wired, but I thought we'd be safe out here.'

Jessica moistened dry lips. 'I'm sure you're mistaken. It was only—'

He held up a hand to silence her. 'Forgive me, dear lady. I know you're trying to soothe me, but it's no use blinking facts.' He turned to right the chair and noted the crack in one of the uprights. 'Shoddy workmanship these days,' he remarked, seemingly oblivious of the fact that he himself had caused the damage. 'No matter, it will still bear my weight. Now, where were we? *Chaste virgin moon,* I believe.'

Jessica gazed at him helplessly, knowing herself to be incapable of continuing. And was saved by the back door opening as Matthew emerged.

'Hello, Leo. Will you join us in a sherry before lunch?'

Leo sprang to his feet with an expression of petulance

at yet another interruption. Fortunately this time it was fleeting.

'Good of you, Matthew, but I must get back. Jessica has honoured my poor offerings, thereby elevating them to the classics!' He took her hand again and kissed it. 'I'll call another time, if I may, and we shall indulge ourselves further. Goodbye, dear lady. My most grateful thanks.'

Matthew opened the side gate for him, then came across to Jessica, his smile fading as he saw her face. 'Darling, whatever is it?'

'He's mad!' she whispered. 'Matthew, he's quite mad.'

He drew her up into his arms, feeling her trembling. 'Tell me what happened.'

Wonderingly, unbelievingly, she did so. 'Heaven help me,' she ended, 'I thought he was a figure of fun. I was laughing to myself about him all the time. Then, suddenly, *that*! It was *horrible*!'

'Poor darling.' Matthew held her close, kissing her hair. 'I did tell you he was unbalanced. I doubt if it's worse than that.'

'But he was so *violent*! If that pilot had been on the ground, Leo would have gone for him, I'm sure. I was terrified'.

'Sweetheart, the world's full of people with a persecution complex. Ask any desk sergeant at a police station. People are always going in and saying their phones are tapped and Big Brother is watching them.'

She shuddered. 'Does his family know he's like that?'

'Oh yes. But he's harmless, really.'

'And then suddenly crying—like a baby. Openly and unashamedly. It was grotesque.'

Matthew led her back to the house. 'We'll have a brandy instead of sherry. That'll steady you. What is it about this garden? You had the jitters last time you were out here.'

'He said he'd come back. I hope to God he doesn't. It was so totally unexpected, the change that came over him. Like—like being bitten by a teddy-bear!'

Carrie turned from the cooker as they entered the kitchen,

her eyes moving over Jessica's face. Had she seen anything from the kitchen window? Jessica could hardly ask her. 'Dinner's ready, mum.'

Matthew smiled at her. 'Thanks, Carrie, but we'll have a drink first. Give us five minutes, will you?' Closing the kitchen door, he turned Jessica to face him. 'All right now?'

'I suppose so. God, what a morning! First the press and then Leo.'

'Don't worry any more. I'll have a discreet word with Dominic. He won't come again.'

'No.' She straightened. 'Don't do that. As you said, no doubt he's harmless, and I don't want to hurt his feelings. Probably no one else has time to listen to him or read his dreadful rhymes.' She paused, then corrected herself. 'Poetry.' She met Matthew's eye and smiled. 'I'm all right. Really. Never mind the brandy, let's have lunch.'

CHAPTER 8

Matthew said, 'You will be all right, won't you?'

'I shall have to be.'

'I was lucky to get this appointment, but if you want me to, I could cancel it.' His tone was indicative of his reaction to such a request. *If I'm made to feel guilty each time I leave you—*

'That's not necessary.'

'I'd suggest your coming too, but the research wouldn't interest you and car journeys are painful for you anyway.'

'What time will you be back?'

'About six, I should think. The museum closes at five-thirty.'

'I thought the Sandons had their family documents at the Hall?'

'Not on Lord Hubert. He was a general in the Napoleonic Wars, mentioned in despatches and so on. As he's a local celebrity, his stuff is in the county museum—diaries, ledgers and lord knows what. I'll have to go through all of them. God knows how long it will take. Ask Carrie to come in and get lunch for you. I'm sure she would.'

'Not on a Wednesday; she helps at the nursing home.' Seeing his flicker of impatience, she added, 'I can manage, don't worry, and I've plenty to be getting on with. I haven't been over my lines yet, and there's that novel you brought from the library.'

He looked relieved. 'Good girl. Just keep the doors locked, and you'll have nothing to worry about.'

Which naturally resurrected her fears. She stood at the door watching him drive off. At the cottage across the road, a man was talking on the step to the young woman who lived there. She was rocking a baby in her arms, patting its back mechanically as she answered his questions. Was he from the press or the police? There was no way of telling. Like a general reviewing a battlefield, Jessica sized up her position. On her left, fields adjoined the garden and there were no near neighbours. There was a house to the right, but she'd never seen the owners. Would anyone hear her, if she screamed?

She shut the door quickly and turned the key. Then, swinging herself on her crutches, she went through to the kitchen and bolted the back door, too. She leant against the sink for a moment, staring out at the garden where, the day before, Leo had disintegrated before her eyes. Suppose he came back today? She wouldn't dare open the door to him, but if he walked round the house looking in windows, there was nowhere she could hide. Had Matthew locked the side gate? If only she could go upstairs unaided! And even if Leo didn't come, she had eight long hours ahead of her, during which she'd be constantly listening for any unexplained sound.

The phone shrilled, making her jump, but when she stumbled to it, precariously leaning forward to lift the receiver, it was only another reporter with the same old questions. Ironically, today she'd have welcomed a visit rather than a phone-call.

A sitting target. The phrase came unbidden into her mind. And it occurred to her suddenly that the murderer—and the rapist, if they weren't the same—would also be reading the newspapers. And would learn that Jessica Randal, incapacitated by a broken leg, was now staying in the murdered woman's cottage.

Didn't the criminal return to the scene of the crime? And the police seemed to think Freda'd been killed here. Why else had the house been given such a going-over? Suppose he decided to kill two birds with one stone? She shivered at the appositeness of the cliché.

She was still by the telephone, and on impulse picked up the directory and flicked through it for Kathy Markham's number. Perhaps she'd be free to come to coffee—even lunch. A simple meal wasn't beyond her capabilities, despite Matthew's insistence on rest. She could follow up her invitation to the daughter at the same time. What was her name? Angie! As if she could forget!

But when the number had been dialled, it rang unanswered in an empty house. Jessica's disappointment was out of all proportion.

As long as you lock the doors, you'll be safe. But what about the windows? It would be simple to break one of their tiny panes and put a hand inside to unlatch them. If this was America, she thought, at least she'd have a gun to protect herself. Everyone did.

She said aloud, 'Don't be a fool. You're not the only woman in this village alone in her house.'

But the only one who'd received so much publicity.

At least no one knew Matthew wasn't home.

Unless they'd been watching the house, and seen him leave. She seemed to be holding a conversation with the two halves of her brain, arguing a case and demolishing it at the same time.

If only she'd someone to talk to—anyone! But there was

no one else she could ring. Certainly not Giselle Sandon; Leo might answer the phone.

Jessica swung restlessly to the window. At the top of its long, sloping garden, the rear windows of The Willows blinked inscrutably back at her. Lucky Carrie, with every minute of her day occupied! Jessica pictured her moving from room to room with her dusters and can of polish, busy, useful—and safe. And suddenly she remembered Lois Winter, whom she'd met at the Markhams' party.

Almost stumbling in her eagerness, she turned back to the phone. The calm, pleasant voice answered at once. 'The Willows Residential Home. Matron speaking.'

'Mrs Winter—it's Jessica Selby.'

Warmth dissipated the professionalism. 'Hello, Mrs Selby. How are you?'

'I'm phoning to offer myself for Good Works. No, don't thank me, this is pure selfishness. I'm going out of my mind, all by myself and thinking of the murder. God knows what I could do without the use of my legs, but there must be *something*. At very least I could sit with someone, if that's any help. Read to them, or write their letters.'

'But of course we'd be delighted to have you. The staff are run off their feet, and despite all the facilities available, some residents are alone too much.'

Only as Jessica released her breath did she realize how tensely she'd awaited Matron's reply. 'Then that's fine,' she said. 'I'm free now, if someone could collect me.'

Webb stood on the steps of the police station and watched the subdued figure of Bruce Cowley walk to his car. Then, with a shrug, he turned and went back inside.

'No joy, Guv?' asked the desk sergeant.

'He's in the clear, Andy. He was at a convention on the fifth—roughly five hundred witnesses. Seemed pretty shattered, too. He reckoned he was still fond of her, though he's not been in touch since he did the bunk. "Always meant to go back one day," he said. Well, hard luck, mate. You left it too late.'

In the general office upstairs, a group of DCs were clustered, laughing, round young Marshbank's desk. Catching sight of Webb, the boy flushed and slid a piece of paper under some files. Webb paused by his desk. 'Well, Simon, can't I share the joke?'

Marshbank's flush deepened. 'It's nothing much, Guv.'

'Go on, Simon,' urged one of the others. 'Let the Governor see it. He could do with a laugh.'

Reluctantly the young man retrieved the paper and handed it over. Written in his cramped hand were several lines of doggerel.

> *Sing a song of murder, a pocketful of rhyme,*
> *Four and twenty coppers try to solve a crime.*
> *When the corpse was spotted, the wires began to buzz.*
> *Wasn't that a dainty dish to set before the Fuzz?*

'Um.' Webb handed it back to him. 'Very neat. Pity the post of Laureate's been filled. Right, that's enough larking about. If you lads have nothing to do, I can soon find you something.'

But he repeated the verse to Crombie with a wry smile in the privacy of his office.

'That nursery rhyme angle's going to be a bind,' the Inspector said gloomily. 'We've already had some comedian on the phone asking to speak to Boy Blue.' He grinned suddenly. 'How about "There came a big *Spider*," eh, Dave?'

'Honestly, Alan, you're as bad as the rest of them.' His phone rang, and he lifted it. 'Webb.'

'About that drink—' said a voice in his ear.

A wave of heat washed over him, as unexpected as it was unwelcome. 'Hello, Susan,' he said flatly.

Behind him, he heard Crombie's chair scrape and the door quietly open and close. He was not sure whether to be grateful or indignant for such obvious tact.

'Are you free tonight?'

Webb hesitated. All his instincts told him it was wiser not to see her, to keep putting her off till she finally gave up bothering. But he heard himself say, 'I could be, though only for an hour or so.'

'Fair enough. What time?'

'Seven?'

'I'll be on the corner.'

She didn't have to specify which one. During their years together, she'd waited many a time for him to pick her up on the corner of Carrington Street, just along from the station. She rang off without awaiting his acknowledgement, and he stood helplessly for a moment, the receiver still to his ear, fighting the nightmare sensation that they were still together, that the five-year gap had never been, that there was no Hannah. Then he dropped the phone, walked round the corner of his desk and sat down heavily in his chair. Well, he'd done it now. He should have stuck to his guns, refused to meet her. But beneath the familiar churning of his stomach was a rising tide of excitement.

Jessica was taken in the lift to the first floor and Matron's room. Lois Winter came to meet her. 'How nice to see you again! Come and have a coffee while we discuss what you should do.'

Jessica's spirits soared. If all went well, she need never spend a day alone at Hinckley's. Any time Matthew was out—even if he remained incommunicado in his study—she could escape to the bustling, friendly atmosphere of The Willows. She gave a sigh of sheer pleasure as, removing her crutches, Lois settled her in a chair with professional efficiency.

Jessica looked about her, admiring the high ceiling and long windows looking down the garden, the pastel walls and the watercolours that hung there. 'What a lovely room.'

'It's my sanctuary. It restores me when I'm in much need of restoration.'

A tap on the door heralded Carrie Speight with the coffee. She looked surprised to see Jessica.

'Mrs Selby's kindly offered us her time,' Lois explained.

As the girl went out, Jessica said, 'She's a quiet little thing, isn't she? Friendly and willing, but so pale.'

Lois nodded. 'She's taken Mrs Cowley's death very badly. I'm a little concerned about her.'

'I hope it doesn't make things worse, coming to Hinckley's to look after us.'

Lois made no reply, leaving Jessica with the impression that she felt it did. But how could they manage without Carrie?

'Now,' Lois was saying, handing her a cup of coffee, 'let me fill you in briefly on the running of the Home. First, you'll have noticed I'm known as Matron. We're old-fashioned in that—none of your modern Nursing Officers here! It reassures the residents—they know where they are with "Matron". We have ten at the moment, a married couple among them. Apart from old Mr Denny, the rest are all ladies. They're in varying states of health, some extremely fit, others less so. Miss Sampson is senile, but perfectly happy. And Mrs Southern is paralysed but as sharp as a pin mentally.' Lois paused. 'Ninety per cent of the time, anyway, though I hear she's started to ramble.

'Each of them has a bedsitting-room furnished with their own possessions, and there's a pleasant lounge with a sun-room attached, when they want to be sociable. We have three trained nurses beside myself, who live in the annexe at the bottom of the garden. Cook and her husband have a flat in the basement, and the cleaners are village women who come in daily. Dr Prentiss calls every Friday, and, of course, on demand at any time. As you probably know, Carrie comes to us at the weekends and spends each Wednesday here, and on alternate weeks her sister comes to do the ladies' hair. I think that's all you need to know, but if you think of anything else, please ask.

'Now to your contribution. Though you can't serve meals,

you might perhaps help with feeding Mrs Southern.'

Seeing Jessica's look of alarm, she added, 'That's not as distressing as it sounds. She has a healthy appetite, enjoys her food, and eats impeccably. In fact, I think Mrs Southern would benefit the most from your company. I should start with her. She's highly intelligent and gets bored with television, which the others tend to leave on all day. She has her radio, but she can't read as much as she'd like, because of difficulty in turning the pages. We've rigged up something for her, but it has its limitations.'

'I'd be glad to help,' Jessica said.

Lois smiled. 'And that beautiful, trained voice of yours will make listening to you an added pleasure. I hope your husband won't mind our borrowing you like this, but when we're offered help of any kind, we seize it with both hands.'

'Matthew's out quite a lot doing his research, and when he's in, he's busy writing. I'm delighted to have something useful to do.' She paused. 'I suppose you knew Mrs Cowley?'

'Only by sight. She was friendly with Kathy Markham, I believe.'

'I keep thinking about her,' Jessica said in a low voice, 'wondering exactly what happened, and where.' She shuddered. 'I woke up in the night, and I suddenly thought— suppose she was killed *in this bed*! It's quite likely, in the circumstances.'

Lois said gently, 'It's upsetting for you, I know. I also know it's useless telling you not to think about it.'

'Do you think he'll—attack again?'

'Mrs Selby, I'm not the police.'

'But medically speaking, you must have some idea.' And as Lois hesitated, she added, 'It's quite likely, isn't it?'

'He could be miles away by now.'

'If so, he'll come back. He must have some connection with the village.'

'We're safe enough as long as we're sensible. And with the village so full of police, any murderer would think twice about coming here. Now, if you've finished your coffee I'll introduce you to Mrs Southern. Her room's just along the corridor.'

Mrs Southern was in her usual place at the window, and as Jessica joined her, she saw Hinckley's Cottage in full view across the lower road. The old lady listened to Matron's explanation, and inclined her head.

'I'll leave you to get to know each other,' Lois finished brightly. 'If you want anything, Mrs Selby, just ring the bell.'

Jessica turned back to find sharp grey eyes examining her. 'You're very beautiful,' Mrs Southern pronounced.

She smiled. 'Thank you.'

'You must be used to being told so. I was, in my young days.' It was said without conceit, a statement of fact, and judging by the bone structure under the velvety old skin, Jessica had no reason to doubt it.

'Have you any children, Mrs Selby?'

'Not of my own. Have you?'

'Two sons and a daughter. They visit me quite regularly —to keep an eye on their money.'

'Oh, I'm sure it isn't that!'

'No,' Mrs Southern agreed, 'I don't suppose it is. They've been good to me.'

'Do they live near?'

'My sons both work in London, but my daughter's in Ashmartin.'

'Where's that?'

The keen old eyes raked her face. 'I'd forgotten you're a stranger here. It's the other side of Shillingham, on the Oxfordshire border. An hour and a half's drive from here.'

'Would you like me to write to them for you?'

'Not just now. Thank you,' she added after a pause. 'Tell me about your life on the stage. It must be fascinating.'

'I love it, yes.' Jessica dipped into her store of theatrical anecdotes, deliberately choosing the more amusing to make the old lady smile, and Mrs Southern listened keenly, occasionally breaking in with pertinent and observant questions.

Both of them were sorry when they were interrupted by a knock on the door. One of the cleaners came in, followed by an elderly man in overalls, bearing a pair of steps.

'Now, Mrs Southern,' the woman began loudly, and Jessica saw the old lady wince. There was nothing wrong with her hearing. 'Mr Chitty here is going to change your light-bulb for you. It wasn't working last night, remember?'

'Of course I remember,' Mrs Southern replied waspishly. 'I reported it myself.'

'Got some company today, I see.' The woman smiled at Jessica and then, with a conspiratorial wink which Mrs Southern couldn't have failed to intercept, turned back to the old lady. 'Seen Santa again, have you?'

Jessica looked in puzzlement from one to the other. An expression of doubt crossed the old face and she remained silent.

'Mrs Southern here thinks it's Christmas,' the woman went on, and Chitty, fiddling with the light-bulb, chuckled appreciatively. Jessica longed to slap them both. 'Thinks we're not letting on, and keeping all her presents for ourselves! Did he have his reindeer with him, then?'

Mrs Southern's head jerked up. 'Don't treat me like an idiot, Dolly,' she said tartly. 'I may be approaching second childhood, but I've not yet reverted to believing in Father Christmas.'

Dolly flushed. 'But you told me—'

'People still *dress up* as Santa Claus, don't they, at Christmas time? That's what I saw—a man in a hooded cloak with a sack on his back. Down there.' And she nodded in the direction of Hinckley's Cottage.

The man up the ladder spoke for the first time. 'But it's only September, love. "Christmas comes but once a year," thank heaven.'

'Then tell him, whoever he was, not me,' Mrs Southern retorted with asperity.

Chitty ponderously descended his ladder and pressed the light switch. The bulb lit up, dim in the sunlit room.

'There you are. All fixed.' And he and Dolly left the room.

Jessica said quickly, 'Where were we? Oh yes, touring with *Twelfth Night*. There was one theatre—'

But her mind wasn't on her words. *When* had Mrs Southern seen 'Santa' coming out of Hinckley's with a sack? Mrs Winter must be told. She'd know how much importance to attach to it. For her part, Jessica'd an uneasy suspicion that Mrs Southern wasn't rambling at all.

Webb saw her as soon as he turned out of the gate, her dress a splash of colour in the evening sunshine. He drew up beside her and as she climbed in, he was aware again of her scent.

'Where shall we go?' He didn't look at her.

'The Nutmeg?'

Damn! He shouldn't have asked. Seems she was bent on a nostalgia trip. The Nutmeg, a couple of miles' drive out of town, was the pub where they'd done their courting and which they'd patronized in the early days of their marriage.

Susan glanced at him, acccurately interpreting his silence. 'It's only a suggestion. If you'd rather not, it's all right by me.'

But if he chose otherwise, she'd read all sorts of reasons into it. Angrily he realized he was already back on the treadmill. If I say or do this, will she think I mean that? It had been one of the more wearing aspects of their life together.

Grimly and in silence he drove to The Nutmeg. Though he'd passed it countless times in the last five years, he'd never been inside. When they'd known it, it had had a shabby, rustic charm. Now, under new management, it had been extended and refurbished, and any lingering ghosts of their former selves well and truly despatched.

In the amber-tinted mirror behind the bar, he watched Susan seat herself at a table. If he were seeing her for the first time, would he fancy her? Or was it the remembrance of happier times that made his body jerk like an exposed nerve?

Two men came into the bar, throwing her an admiring glance as they passed. Webb sighed, paid for the drinks, and carried them across to join her. She had already lit a cigarette and the familiar irritation pricked at him as she flicked it in the vague direction of the ashtray and ash fell on the table. A non-smoker himself, her chain-smoking was a longstanding cause of friction and he was grateful, in the ambivalent present, to be reminded of it. On her little finger the amethyst ring glowed softly. It was the only one she wore. Sourly, he wondered what she'd done with her wedding rings.

'Do you know where I went today?' she asked, breaking the silence between them. 'Twenty-three, Priory Gardens.'

He made no comment.

'It was the oddest feeling. The number of times I've walked up that path! They've built on a carport, did you know? And the woodwork's green now. I preferred it blue.'

'Houses change, as people do.'

'I suppose so. I should have known it never pays to go back.'

'Yet you came back to Shillingham.'

'Yes.' She looked at him under lowered lids. 'You've not forgiven me for that, have you? Why? Do you feel threatened by my being here?'

'No, merely curious.' It wasn't true. He felt a positive turmoil of emotions, but he wasn't going to tell her. Anyway, he hadn't identified them all himself.

'I've had a nomadic life, remember. I lived in Shillingham longer than anywhere else, and I needed familiar surroundings.'

'Do you propose to stay?'

'It depends.'

'On what?'

Her eyes held his over the rim of her glass. 'On whether your attitude drives me away.'

'My dear Susan, my "attitude", as you call it, needn't concern you at all. If you hadn't sought me out, I wouldn't even have known you were back.' He paused. 'But you wanted me to know, didn't you?'

'I suppose I must have.'

'If the rape hadn't happened, you'd have found some other reason to come and see me.'

'Probably.'

'Why?'

'Curiosity,' she answered in her turn, and if, like him, she was less than truthful, he couldn't accuse her of it.

'And is it now satisfied?'

'Partly. I wanted to see if you'd changed. You haven't— not really. And I wondered if, now things have died down a bit, we could be friends. Lots of divorced couples are.'

He didn't speak.

'Now, I'm not so sure. Either that we could be friends, or that things have died down.' She gave a small laugh into his continuing silence. 'I must say, you're not very communicative.'

'What do you want me to say?'

'Whether you'd like me to stay.'

'In Shillingham? It's entirely up to you. As you pointed out, I don't own the bloody town.'

'But you'd like me to keep out of your way.'

'I think it would be best. We seem unable to help hurting each other.'

She sighed and finished her drink. 'You're probably right.'

'Another?'

'No. You said you couldn't spare long, and there doesn't seem much else to say.'

A bone-weary sadness seeped over him. 'Susie—'

Her hand clenched on the table, then relaxed. 'It's a long time since anyone called me that.' She stood up abruptly. 'Let's go.'

Dusk was deepening as they drove back along the country road to the lights of Shillingham. 'Where are you staying?'

'Drop me in Gloucester Circus—that's near enough.'

'No, I'll take you to your door. Where is it?'

'Park Road. Number nineteen.'

There were houses on only one side of Park Road, small semi-detacheds for the most part. Opposite them, darkness was already among the trees of the park.

'It's the white house, past the next lamp-post.'

He drew up and she waited impassively while he got out and opened the door for her. In silence he escorted her up the short path, as, he remembered unwillingly, he had done up her parents' path during their engagement. At the door she turned with a bright smile.

'Well, it was nice knowing you, as they say.'

He stood looking at her, trying to think of a suitable reply. The misery was as intense as he remembered. He hadn't expected to feel it again.

'Good night, Susie.'

He wasn't sure which of them moved, but suddenly they were straining together, her mouth avidly seeking his as her hands dug into his hair, forcing him even closer. He held on to her, the remembered intimacy of her igniting bones and blood with insatiable urgency. Her mouth, her full, sensual mouth, with its lingering taste of tobacco.

With a strength he didn't know he possessed, he wrenched himself free, gasping in draughts of cool air. She said, 'Dave!' Then, rapidly, 'Dave, Dave, Dave!'

He turned and stumbled back down the path. She made no attempt to stop him. He started the car, drove it for some yards down the road, then stopped again, gripping the steering-wheel.

He was a bloody fool to meet her. He should have guessed what would happen. Nothing had changed. They were still poles apart mentally and obsessed with each other's bodies. It would be no different from before.

During their last months together, they'd made love in anger, in bitterness, resenting their physical need of each other which took no account of the emotional scratchiness which was driving them apart. Then, when she'd gone, he'd endured nearly three years of celibacy. He didn't care for casual sex, nor was it open to one of his calling. Police Regulations saw to that.

He drew a deep breath. Her scent, newly remembered, still lingered in the car, bringing back not the stressful end of their marriage, but the times when last it had come fresh to his nostrils—their first few meetings, all those years ago. And he knew, despairingly, that if the chance offered, he would make love to her.

And Hannah? He felt a stab of guilt. Hannah was sanity, tenderness, comfort: Susie irritation and unhealthy obsession. He'd thought that after all this time he could handle it, and he'd been wrong. God knew where it would end.

He straightened, staring down the darkening road ahead of him. In the trees of the park an owl hooted. He turned the ignition key and the car moved slowly on down the road.

CHAPTER 9

Kathy said gently, 'You really should go home, you know. You don't look at all well.'

Carrie shook her head, wiping her hand across her mouth. 'I'll be all right, mum.'

'Is it your tooth again?'

'No. I—I ate something that upset me.'

'Then you should be in bed, not rushing about here with the Hoover. You need time to get over it.'

Carrie gripped the edge of the sink, her head bent over it. 'Please, Mrs Markham, let me stay. I'll—' She broke off, catching her lip between her teeth. Then, as Kathy watched in consternation, she crumpled, bowed over the sink as an avalanche of tears overcame her.

'Carrie! Oh, Carrie, love. Come and sit down.' Kathy

prised her fingers off the sink and led her to a chair. Carrie slumped forward on to the table, her head in her arms.

'There's something else, too, isn't there? Can't you tell me? Perhaps I can help.'

'No one can,' Carrie said with finality. She sat up, reached in her apron for a handkerchief, and blew her nose. 'I'm sorry, mum. I'll be all right now.'

'But there might be something I can do.'

'No, really.' Carrie hesitated, then raised her swollen face to Kathy's. 'I'm going to have a baby.'

Kathy stared at her blankly. She'd never heard Carrie's name linked with an admirer. In her busy life, there didn't seem time for one.

'Are you sure? Have you seen the doctor?'

'I'm sure. I don't need the doctor to tell me that. It's morning sickness, you see.'

'Does your boyfriend know?'

Carrie bit her lip.

'Surely he'd help you? Or is he already married?'

'Oh mum, you don't understand!' The tears came again. Carrie covered her face with her handkerchief, rocking backwards and forwards in inconsolable grief.

Oh *God*! Why hadn't she realized? Kathy knelt beside her and took her hand. 'Carrie, you were raped, weren't you?' The sobs continued unabated. 'When was it? How long ago? Have you told Matron?'

But Carrie, apparently regretting her confidence, resisted all attempts to make her elaborate. She was pregnant, and that's all she'd admit to. Patently, she regretted having gone that far. Regaining a precarious control, she gave Kathy a firm if watery smile and left the room.

The police should be told, Kathy thought uneasily. This extra evidence might be vital. Lois would know what to do. Yet even telling Lois seemed a betrayal of confidence.

After weighing the matter for some minutes, Kathy reached her usual conclusion. She would wait till Guy came home, and see what he thought. And with her course of action decided, she collected her shopping basket and thankfully left the house.

Jessica was reading to Mrs Southern when the police arrived.

'It's all right, Mrs Selby,' the Chief Inspector said. 'No need for you to go.' He felt the old lady would be more relaxed with someone familiar in the room. Matron, too, had followed him to the door. 'Chief Inspector Webb, ma'am, Shillingham CID. Now—' he drew up a chair—'I believe you saw someone from your window here, someone acting suspiciously. Is that right?'

Mrs Southern said clearly, 'Are you trying to have me certified, Matron?'

Webb looked startled and Lois came quickly into the room, but it was Jessica who answered. 'Quite the opposite, Mrs Southern. It's because we're sure you *did* see someone that Matron asked the Inspector to come.'

The old lady looked from one to the other. 'Father Christmas?' she inquired drily.

Webb said, 'Could you tell me when this was, ma'am?'

She studied him for a moment, then, deciding he was genuinely interested, paused to consider. 'It was the day Mrs Parbold was taken ill.'

Webb looked at Lois and raised his eyebrows.

'About a fortnight ago. I can check.'

'A Wednesday,' Mrs Southern put in. 'I remember, because Carrie was here. She gave me my supper.'

'Wednesday, a fortnight ago.' Almost certainly the day of the murder. 'And what time would it be, ma'am?'

'Quite late. It was starting to get dark.'

'That's right,' Lois confirmed. 'Normally we put Mrs Southern to bed before the day staff go off duty, and she has supper in bed. But that day everything was delayed because of the emergency.'

'So what time *was* supper served?'

'About seven-thirty, I suppose.'

Webb stood up and looked down the length of the garden to Hinckley's Cottage. 'It's quite a distance, Mrs Southern. Are you quite sure about what you saw?'

'There's nothing wrong with my eyesight, Chief Inspector,' she answered crisply. 'It compensates for my other disabilities.' She glanced without emotion at the useless hands in her lap. 'However, if you'd like a demonstration: a car's just drawn into the drive down there, and a gentleman with fair hair is getting out. He's wearing a brown jacket and flannel trousers.'

'I'm impressed,' Webb conceded, watching Matthew Selby go into the house. 'So now we come to the crux. What exactly did you see, that Wednesday evening?'

'The house was in darkness, that was what interested me. I'm a nosey old lady, Chief Inspector, with little to do but sit here all day. I know who lives in all the houses along there, what time they go out and when they return. Gentlemen frequently call at that cottage, but I was surprised to see one emerge when no lights had been on.'

'How clearly could you see him?'

'Not clearly at all, but there's a street lamp at the gate.'

'Can you describe him?'

'No. He was bending forward, with a sack over his shoulder. It seemed to be quite heavy.'

'Was he as tall as the gentleman we've just seen?'

She considered. 'I don't think so.'

Jessica sent Webb a triumphant glance, but it was premature. Mrs Southern added: 'Of course, with his stooping it's difficult to be certain.'

'You couldn't see the colour of his hair?'

'No, he was wearing a hood or cloak of some kind.' She paused. 'My confusion, Chief Inspector, was due to my being upset. I was worried about Mrs Parbold, the routine to which I'm so accustomed had been disrupted, and I felt—disorientated. Which was what led to the foolishness about Santa Claus. But it undoubtedly looked like him.'

'So he came out of the front door carrying a sack. What colour was it?'

'Black.' No hesitation that time.

'And what did he do with it?'

'He put it in the boot of the car. Then he went back and collected a suitcase, pulled the door shut, and drove off.'

'Had you seen the car before?'

'Oh yes, it was always in the drive.'

'Now, Mrs Southern. You say you often saw gentlemen come and go. Did you notice that one arrive?'

'I'm afraid not.'

'But you'd been at the window all day.'

'Yes, but I have a little nap, you see, after my lunch. I saw the lady who lived there go out, while Nurse was helping me with my meal. But I didn't see her come back.'

'So she might have returned with this man soon after lunch, while you were having your nap?'

'She might.'

Jessica's heart was thudding against her ribcage. He was thinking of Matthew and Mrs Cowley at The Orange Tree. 'Or,' she said, surprising them, 'she could have gone back alone, and the man arrived later.'

'True.' Webb considered for a moment, tugging at his lip. 'Would you recognize any of the gentlemen you'd seen going to that house?'

'I might. There was a tall one, I remember, who walked like a soldier.'

'But you don't know if you'd seen the one with the sack before?'

'Regretfully, no.' She paused. 'I don't see the papers, Chief Inspector—they're too difficult for me to manage— but I listen to the news on the wireless. Do you believe what I saw was the murderer leaving with that poor woman's body?'

'I believe it might well have been, ma'am.'

*

'Not much wrong with that one's brain,' Webb told Jackson, who'd awaited him in the car. 'Too bad she wasn't still at her window the night of the rape. We'd probably have had him by now.'

'Talking of which, Guv, a message just came over the radio. The results from the first batch of blood samples are in, and there's a non-secretor among them.'

'Who, Ken?'

'One of the mob up at the Hall. A Mr Leo Sandon.'

'Well, well. Then let us make our way there without delay and have a word with the gentleman.'

'Inspector Crombie says his alibi was weak, too. He went out after dinner but just "wandered about", he said.'

'There are three lads there, too, don't forget. Rather a wild bunch, from all accounts.'

'Half French,' confirmed Jackson, with an endemic distrust of foreigners. 'Look—isn't that Miss Speight, hurrying down the hill?'

'So it is. Slow down, Ken, would you.' Webb wound down his window and Carrie, turning when she heard the car, started as she recognized its occupants.

'Good morning, Miss Speight.' She nodded silently. 'Remembered anything else that might help us? Anything missing from the cottage that you forgot to mention?'

'Well, there was the rubber gloves, sir. It's probably not important, and I forgot about them because I bought a new pair straight after. But the ones that hung over the sink—Mrs Cowley's, like—they'd disappeared.'

There'd been a suggestion of rubber on the typewriter keys. Crafty bugger, Jackson thought with unwilling admiration.

Webb nodded. 'Anything else?'

'I don't think so, sir.'

'Well, let us know if you remember anything, however unimportant it may seem.'

'Yes, sir.' She stood looking after them as the car moved away down the hill.

'You know what I told you about Millie, Guv?' Jackson said slowly.

'That she's going to make you a father again?'

'Yes. Well, that Miss Speight's got the same look about her, round the eyes. Wouldn't surprise me if she's in the family way.'

'Nonsense, Ken. You've got babies on the brain.'

The Honourable Leo Sandon baffled the policemen. With a great show of cooperation, he told them nothing. 'You see, Superintendent—' (Webb let that pass)—'when I'm composing, I'm unaware of my surroundings. I wander as the muse takes me, registering only fleeting impressions of my whereabouts as they impinge on my poetry.'

'I see, sir,' Webb said stolidly. 'Verse you write, is it? But you'd know if you wandered as far as the village, surely?'

'But you see, Superintendent,' Leo insisted earnestly, 'one day is much like another as far as I'm concerned. I'm not at all clear which day you're interested in, and even if I were, I shouldn't be able to distinguish it after all this time.'

'Nutty as a fruit-cake,' Jackson said gloomily on the way back to Shillingham, and Webb was inclined to agree.

Jessica told Matthew of Webb's visit as he drove her home from The Willows. 'That window's like a lookout post,' she said. 'We watched you get out of the car and go into the house.'

'Just as well I hadn't a sack over my shoulder.'

'Don't joke about it, Matthew.' She was remembering the old lady's nap, during which both Mrs Cowley and her murderer had entered the cottage, either separately or together.

'Carrie arrived as I was leaving to fetch you,' he added. 'Steak for supper this evening.'

'I could take over the cooking now, you know.'

'But why should you, as long as she's prepared to do it? And she's probably glad of the extra cash.'

'What did you have for lunch?'

'I opened a can of beans.'

'Oh, darling! I could come back and see to it when Carrie's not there.'

'I shan't starve. I'm more concerned about your taking on too much up there. I'd have thought half a day was enough.'

'We'll see how it goes,' Jessica said diplomatically.

When they reached the cottage, Matthew returned to his study and Jessica went to the kitchen. Carrie was peeling potatoes at the sink. She looked paler than ever, and her eyes were red-rimmed as though she'd been weeping. Was she still grieving for Mrs Cowley, or had something else upset her?

'Hello, Carrie,' she said with false heartiness. 'Everything all right?'

Carrie nodded, pushing her hair off her face with the back of her hand.

'I was saying to my husband, I'm perfectly capable of taking over the cooking now, if you'd like to stop. It must be a tie coming here so often—we do appreciate what you've done.'

'It's no trouble, mum,' Carrie said dully.

'You're quite happy to continue?'

'If you'd like me to.'

There was a brief silence. Carrie went on with the potatoes while Jessica cast round for another topic of conversation. And found one.

'By the way, I've been meaning to ask you. Do you think your sister would come and wash my hair for me?'

'Yes, mum, of course.'

'It doesn't need setting, but though I've tried to wash it, I can't manage very well.'

'Della'd do it. She often goes to ladies' houses.'

'Then would you ask her, please?'

That, Jessica thought with satisfaction, would complete her wellbeing. With clean hair and her days safely occupied, she could look life in the eye again. And as if to test her, the phone rang.

Carrie looked up, but Jessica turned to the door. 'It's all right, I'll take it.'

A woman's voice said hesitatingly, 'May I speak to Matthew Selby, please?'

'Of course. Who shall I say?'

The briefest of pauses. Then, 'Angela.'

For the space of a second the name meant nothing. Then realization came, and with it apprehension. 'Just a moment.' She was actress enough to allow no tremor in her voice. She swung to the study door and opened it. Matthew looked up, a frown between his eyes.

'Sorry to disturb you,' she said lightly. 'Your ex is on the phone.'

'Damnation!' He rose quickly, brushed past her in the doorway, and lifted the receiver. Jessica leant against the lintel, watching him.

'Angie?' He'd turned slightly away from her, as though to exclude her from their conversation. She studied dispassionately the set of his shoulders, the fair head bent attentively to his ex-wife's voice. 'No, I hadn't forgotten.' A pause. 'Yes, I should think so, if it means so much to her. It's only a couple of hours' drive . . . At the Carlton?'

Jessica could hear the low hum of the woman's voice over the wires, without being able to distinguish the words. Matthew turned, meeting her eyes though still mentally linked to Angie. 'That sounds a sensible arrangement. Will you make the reservation, and I'll confirm it in writing. Thanks. I'll see you then.'

He put the phone down and Jessica stood motionless, waiting. 'It's my daughter's birthday a week on Saturday,' he said. 'She wants me at her party.'

'Oh.'

'It's being held at a local hotel; Angie suggests I spend the night there afterwards. You'd be all right for one night, wouldn't you?'

'I suppose so. I hope the murderer's caught by then.'

'If you're nervous, ask Carrie to sleep in the spare room.'

Jessica said lightly, 'Angie phoning reminds me I've not asked the other Angie over, as I promised. She'll be back at school now, so it will have to be a Saturday.'

'I'll keep out of the way, then. She won't want to see me.'

'You must put in an appearance, at least, or she'll think you're avoiding her.'

'I should be!' He came across and put an arm round her. 'Darling, I'm sorry. Ever since we arrived here, I've been behaving like a bear with a sore head. You're probably regretting having married me.'

'I wouldn't say that.' She turned and regarded him with her strange, slate-coloured eyes. 'Though I *have* wondered what was wrong.'

'A couple of minor matters, like rape and murder. Nothing to worry about.'

'You don't really think Webb suspects you?' But she wondered herself, especially after that morning.

'I don't know what the hell he thinks. The point is, everything was all right until we arrived, whereupon mayhem promptly broke out.'

'Our sense of timing could have been better. On the other hand, if the murder hadn't happened, the cottage wouldn't have become vacant and we shouldn't be here at all.'

'Quite.' He hesitated, not looking at her. 'The reason for my ill-temper, though, is rather more personal. I want like hell to make love to you, and the frustration's building all the time.'

She slid an arm round his neck. 'I want it, too.'

'That bloody copper even suggested it was a motive for rape.'

'Matthew! You never told me that!'

'Of course I didn't. I shouldn't have told you now, but I felt I owed you an explanation.'

'I'm seeing the consultant tomorrow. Perhaps there'll be better news then.'

They moved apart as Carrie came in with a tray, feeling closer than they had for some time.

'What bloody rotten luck,' Crombie said. 'Will she have an abortion?'

'God knows. That at least isn't our pigeon. Hell, Alan, I'm beginning to wonder how many rapes there've been. We'd never have heard of this one, but for the pregnancy. As it was, Matron had a job getting her to report it.'

'Did anything new emerge?'

'No, she was pretty unforthcoming. Made Sally wait till she'd cooked Selby's lunch, if you please. Even then she didn't want to talk, and when she finally did, it was just a repetition of the other cases—woollen helmet and so on. Except for one thing. She didn't mention the nursery rhymes till Sally asked outright. And that really upset her.'

'Well, it would. In nine months she'll be saying them again, and it'll bring it all back.'

'Yep. I didn't think of that. So that's three rapes we know about, and one murder, and we're no nearer catching him than we were ten days ago. Let's hope to God it doesn't take another before we can nab him.'

Della arrived with Carrie that evening. 'I hear you want a shampoo,' she said. 'I can do it now, if it's convenient.'

'Oh. Yes, thank you.' Jessica glanced at Carrie, who, with a strained smile, moved past her and went to the kitchen. 'The cloakroom basin won't be big enough,' she added. 'We'll have to use the bathroom.'

'Righty-ho.' Della was looking about her with bright, inquisitive eyes.

'Perhaps you could help me. I've been given a new, lighter plaster today, but I'm still nervous of steps.'

'Sure.' Side by side they made their way up the steep stairs and into the bathroom. So this was Della Speight. More attractive than Carrie, with those deep blue eyes and curly hair, but there was something about her Jessica didn't take to.

'I didn't know what shampoo you liked, so I brought a selection. The herbal's very good.'

'That'll be fine.'

Della had moved the bathroom chair to the basin and opened the holdall she'd brought with her. Out of it she took an overall, which she slipped on as she talked. 'Pretty hair you've got, haven't you? Well cut, too. Bet that cost you a bomb!'

'It only needs cutting every six weeks. Unless I'm working, I wash it myself, but I haven't been able to manage since the accident.'

'I hear you go up to The Willows,' Della said chattily, shampooing Jessica's head with professional speed. 'Hardly a bundle of laughs, is it?'

'I've only met Mrs Southern so far. She's a charming old lady.'

'A sharp tongue, though. I do her hair, and it has to be just so.' She gave a contemptuous little laugh. 'Her and her Father Christmas!'

'But she did see someone,' Jessica defended her. 'The police think it might be important.'

'More fools them. She doesn't know if it's Monday or Christmas, that one, for all her snappy answers. Mind you, Miss Sampson's worse. Completely off her head. Wait till you see her.'

'I'm surprised you go up there, if you dislike it so much.' Jessica hoped the towel had muffled some of her asperity. Della gave no sign of noticing it.

'Well, it's the money, isn't it? They pay full rates. Mind you, they can afford it. And it's only once a fortnight, on my half day. Keeps me in ciggies, if nothing else.'

The shampoo finished, they moved to the bedroom, where Della completed her work with a blow-dry. Jessica had to admit she was good.

'That's lovely, Miss Speight,' she said in genuine pleasure

as Della put away her equipment. 'Thank you very much.'

'We ought to get the press back for a photo. "Hair by Della Speight"! I can come any time, just tell Carrie if you want me.'

Matthew came out of the study as the two of them negotiated the stairs, and Jessica introduced him.

Della looked him up and down with her bold eyes, but all she said was, 'I'll see if Carrie's ready to come home.'

'Are you pleased with it?' Matthew asked, as she disappeared into the kitchen.

'Yes, very. I'm not sure about Della, though. She's quite different from Carrie.'

'Yes. I've a feeling if she'd been the one to show up that first day, we'd have looked elsewhere.'

Della reappeared. 'She's not finished yet, so I'll go on ahead. That's five pounds, Mrs Selby, including VAT.'

'Let me.' Matthew stepped forward.

'Ta. Well, see you again sometime.'

'Quite a glamour puss, isn't she, that Mrs Selby of yours?'

'I suppose so,' Carrie said listlessly.

'Too bad she's not a regular. I could make a name for myself. We'll feel the pinch when they go, and your extra cash dries up. How long do you reckon you can go on working?'

Carrie turned her head away, lips trembling.

'Oh, come on! It's not the end of the world. Lots of women'd give their souls for a kid.'

'But not this way! Not like this!'

'You shouldn't take risks, I'm always telling you. Hey, I've just thought! What if Sister's been caught, too? That'd be a laugh!'

Carrie spun round. 'A *laugh*? Is that what you call it? You think it's a joke?'

'All right, calm down—I didn't mean you. But you like kids, and no one's going to blame you for what's happened, so why not try and make the best of it?'

Carrie drew a deep breath. 'Yes,' she said, 'I expect you're right. I'll go and get supper.'

CHAPTER 10

Angie Markham ran down the path and turned at the gate to wave. Matthew closed the door. 'Pretty little thing, isn't she?'

'Yes, and she'll make a good actress, too, if she gets the right training. She has a natural flair.' Jessica put an arm round his waist. 'Thanks for putting in an appearance, darling. And you needn't have worried about her not liking you.'

'A forgiving nature. As has her mother, since we're invited to dinner. Unfortunately I have to go to Oxford on Tuesday and might be late back. Perhaps we could ask the other guests to collect you, and I'll get there as soon as I can.'

Jessica grimaced. 'My friend Charles Palmer!'

'He won't proposition you if his wife's there!'

'I can cope with propositions, as long as that's all he tries.'

Matthew frowned. 'You're still casting him as murderer? Isn't that rather stretching it?'

'Potential murderer, and it's not stretching it at all. It has to be *someone*, Matthew, and in all probability we've met him. It hardly encourages one to feel sociable.'

Michael Romilly looked up as the door burst open and Jill came storming into his office.

'Have you seen this?' She slammed a copy of the *Weekly News* on his desk.

'Surprisingly enough, I have.'

'You sanctioned it?'

He tipped his chair back, studying her flushed face. 'Jill, I've no time for guessing games. What are you getting at?'

'Well, look at it!' She jabbed her finger on the front page headlines. 'I don't know about you, but I call that bloody irresponsible!'

He hadn't heard her swear before, and his eyebrow lifted. '"Old lady may have seen murderer,"' he read aloud. 'Is that what's bothering you?'

'Of course it is. Don't you realize it makes her a prime target?'

'Now look: as I understand it, said old lady is cocooned in an old people's home. Short of being locked up in Strangeways, she could hardly be better guarded. No one can get at her.'

'I bet he'll have a damn good try.'

'Bill knows what he's doing.'

'Huh!'

'Could this be professional jealousy, by any chance?'

'No, it couldn't. That's the least of my worries.'

'You did your splurge on the Randal woman.'

'She hadn't seen anything suspicious. She's safe enough.'

'In my opinion, no one in the whole damn village is safe. They've got a right nutter there. Nursery rhymes! Ye gods!'

'I still think that'll put the wind up him. Then who knows what he'll do?'

'If he does anything at all, you'll have my apology in writing.'

'A fat lot of good that'll do the old lady.' She turned on her heel and slammed out of the room. Michael sat looking thoughtfully after her. Then, with a shrug, he turned back to his report.

Susan said, 'Would you rather I didn't talk about it?'

Frances Daly shrugged and reached for the menu. 'Everyone else does. Why should you be any different?' She looked up, meeting her friend's eye. 'Or have you inside information?'

'Afraid not. Dave's playing this one close to his chest.'

'You have seen him, then?'

'We had a drink together.'

'Sounds civilized.'

'But it wasn't. We were both uptight.'

'All the same, I can't imagine Steve and me ever meeting for a drink. What was it like, being with him again?'

Susan played with the pepper mill. 'I still fancy him, Fran.'

'Ah. And is it mutual?'

'I think so.'

'Any chance you'll get back together?'

Susan shrugged. 'I don't think he'd risk it.'

'But you would, given the chance?'

'Oh hell, I don't know. Life with Tony showed up all Dave's good points, but we still irritate each other. He can't stand me smoking, for one thing.'

'Nor can I!'

'Sorry!' Susan stubbed out her cigarette. 'We seem to be talking about me rather than you! Have *you* seen Dave again?'

'He came back on Thursday, to talk to Mrs Southern.'

'Oh yes, I saw that in the paper. Do you think she really saw something?'

'Search me. The police are taking it seriously. It was Mrs Selby who picked it up—Jessica Randal, you know.'

'I read that too. What was she doing with the old woman?'

'She comes up most days to sit with her.'

'Nothing better to do, I suppose. What's she like?'

'Very pleasant. A bit on edge, I'd say.'

'So should I be, living in a dead woman's house.'

A waitress came to take their order, and as she moved away, Susan said curiously, 'You haven't the slightest idea who it could have been? You must know most people in the village.'

'That's what's so horrible. I try them out in my mind, one after the other. Could it be him? Or him? Look, Sue, I'm sorry. Can we change the subject? I'm not quite as blasé as I thought. Have another go at that ex-husband of yours.'

'Don't worry,' Susan said quietly, 'I intend to.'

The cottage was filled with sunshine and the sound of church bells, and Jessica hummed as she prepared lunch. Matthew was up at the Hall this morning, but he'd be back by one, and had promised to spend the rest of the day with her. They might go for a short drive.

As the potatoes came to the boil, the phone rang. She turned down the light and dried her hands on her apron. Probably Matthew, asking her to put lunch back half an hour. Carefully, moving from one piece of furniture to the next for support, she went to answer it.

'Hello?'

There was a click in her ear, followed by a few notes of music and then a man's voice, loudly pitched:

> *'Curly locks, Curly locks,*
> *Wilt thou be mine?*
> *Thou shalt not wash dishes*
> *Nor yet feed the swine,*
> *But sit on a cushion*
> *And sew a fine seam,*
> *And feed upon strawberries,*
> *Sugar and cream.'*

Jessica stood rigid, the phone welded to her ear. Though she longed to drop it, she was incapable of moving. Another tune jingled briefly, then the same voice continued:

> *'Mary, Mary, quite contrary,*
> *How does your garden grow?*
> *With silver bells and cockle shells*
> *And pretty maids all in a row.'*

A crackle came over the wire, then the last line was repeated: *'And pretty maids all in a row.'*

Still Jessica waited, incapable of ending her ordeal. A

further snatch of music introduced *'Where are you going to, my pretty maid?'* When it came to an end, there was a final click and the line buzzed in her ear as, somewhere, a receiver was dropped into place.

Holding her mind suspended, she dialled the number of the Hall which, their first week in the cottage, Matthew had scribbled down in case she needed him. It was the cultured voice of the Dowager which answered.

'Good morning, Mrs Selby. I'm afraid your husband isn't here. He left about half an hour ago.'

'Did he say where he was going?'

'Just a minute.' The phone was covered. A muffled voice called a query, a distant voice replied. Jessica waited, motionless. 'Hello? No, my son understood he was going straight home. No doubt he'll be with you any minute.'

'Thank you.' Jessica replaced the phone, fastidiously wiping her hand on her apron. Where was he? It took only ten minutes to drive back from the Hall. Her brain was still working in the rhythm of the rhymes. *'Thou shalt not wash dishes—'* Where had she heard that recently?

Matthew! He'd recited it when they first arrived here. What a perfectly horrible coincidence. If, said a little voice in her head, it really *was* a coincidence.

She felt suddenly sick. Catching up the phone again, she dialled the operator. 'Get me the police,' she said hoarsely. 'I don't know the number.'

She was talking to Webb when Matthew arrived. She said into the phone, 'My husband's just come in. Thank you, I'll be waiting.'

'Who was that?' When she didn't immediately reply, he looked at her more closely and his voice sharpened. 'Jessica, what is it? What's happened?'

'Where have you been?'

He stopped on his way across to her. 'You know perfectly well where I've been.'

'You left the Hall half an hour ago.'

'Must I account for every minute?'

'Yes, I think you must.' She was having trouble with her breathing.

'Jessica, what the hell is this?'

'Someone phoned and recited a string of nursery rhymes at me.'

'My God!' Then the implication of her attitude came through to him, and his face whitened. 'You don't imagine I . . .?'

'One of them,' she said with dry lips, 'was about not washing dishes nor feeding the swine.'

'So?'

She raised trembling hands to her face. 'Oh Matthew! That's what you said, remember? When we first arrived here?'

'Which makes me a murderer?' Anger overcame his disbelief.

'No, no of course not. But for God's sake, where were you?'

'Not,' he said in a clipped voice, 'in a telephone-box.' He stared back into her wide eyes and added flatly, 'You'd better sit down before you fall down.'

He helped her into a chair. 'As it happens, I was walking in the woods. How's that for a cast-iron alibi? Not that I expected to need one, with you.'

'I'm sorry,' she whispered.

'On the way home, a squirrel dashed across the road in front of me and shot up a tree. I jammed on the brakes, and more or less on impulse got out of the car, but I couldn't see it at first. Then I caught sight of it, or another one, racing along the ground, so I followed it for a while, enjoying the crackle of the leaves under my feet and the sunlight through the branches. I'm sorry. If I'd come straight back, I'd have been here and probably taken the call.'

'How could you know?'

'How indeed?' He went to the sideboard and poured them both a drink. 'I suppose it was friend Webb you were speaking to? He'll be intrigued to know I wasn't where I was supposed to be.'

'I didn't tell him.' This couldn't be happening. He was her *husband*, this hard-eyed stranger whom she'd practically accused of murder.

'Did you mention I'd serenaded you with *Curly locks*?'

'Of course not.'

'Then please don't. He's suspicious enough as it is.' He drained his glass. 'This bloody place! What's it doing to us? We're treating each other like enemies.'

She made a sound and reached out a hand. He gripped it tightly. 'Darling, I'm sorry. I was just so terrified I didn't know what I was doing.'

With his other hand he tipped back her head, forcing her eyes to meet his. 'You didn't really think it was me?'

'Of course not.'

'Darling, I *love* you! Why should I put the fear of God into you?'

'I said I didn't—'

'But you wondered. Even if only briefly.'

To her shame she could not deny it. He gave a brief laugh and dropped her hand. 'And who can blame you? I did lunch with the victim the day she was killed.'

'Stop it, Matthew.'

'Well, at least let's get our story straight. You rang the Hall, presumably, and they said I'd been gone half an hour. Which they'll repeat to the police when they check.'

'You can't blame me for phoning.' Jessica heard her voice rise. 'I needed to speak to you.'

He turned suddenly, sniffing. 'What's that smell?'

'Oh God, the potatoes! They'll have boiled dry.'

'I'll see to it.' He went through to the kitchen, and the burning odour intensified. She heard him open the back door and tip the blackened vegetables into the bin, and the hiss of water running into the burnt pan. After a minute he returned.

'Don't bother doing more. I doubt if either of us has much appetite.'

'There's a joint in the oven.'

His mind had moved on. 'What kind of voice was it?'

'A trained one. An actor's voice. But it must have been on a cassette, because there was music.'

Twenty minutes later, Webb agreed with her. 'He wouldn't risk speaking, other than in a whisper. He must have played a children's cassette over the phone.'

'But why?'

'To frighten you, Mrs Selby. Possibly to warn you.' He paused. 'Which rhymes did he play? Had they anything in common?'

'Only that they were about women,' Jessica said, avoiding Matthew's eye. '*Curly locks, Where are you going to, my pretty maid?* and *Mary, Mary.*' She added shakily, 'I think you're right—he *was* trying to make a point. He played the last line twice: *Pretty maids all in a row.*'

And he had indeed had quite a row of them, Webb thought grimly. 'We can put a recorder on your phone,' he said aloud, 'but it's a bit late for that now. Did you hear any coins being inserted?'

'No, but he could have done it before I answered.'

'I think we must assume that whoever it was knew you were alone. And since your husband would normally be at home on a Sunday morning—'

'He must have seen Matthew leave?'

'Very likely.'

'But damn it, Chief Inspector, I'd been gone an hour and a half. If I hadn't stopped unexpectedly, I *should* have been home.'

'Then he may simply have noticed the car wasn't there, and decided to put the plan into effect.'

'So he must live quite near?'

'In the village, certainly, but as we know from Mrs Southern, this cottage is visible over quite a large area.'

Webb turned to Matthew. 'You mentioned being late home, sir. Why was that?'

Calmly, holding the policeman's eye, he repeated his account of his ill-timed walk.

Webb made no comment, but turned back to Jessica. 'Unless our man was alone in the house, he'll have used a call-box. There are only two in the village, one outside The Orange Tree and the other on the top road near The Willows.'

'Almost opposite here, in fact.'

'Quite. I'd say that was the more likely.'

'But wouldn't it be a risk, in broad daylight, to play a cassette into the mouthpiece?'

'You can get pretty small ones now. If he had it in a paper bag, say, on top of the instrument, it wouldn't be visible to anyone passing, and in any case there's no footpath on that side of the road.'

'He might have been seen entering or leaving the kiosk,' Jackson put in. They all turned to him, having almost forgotten his presence. 'By someone on their way to The Packhorse, for instance, for a lunch-time drink.'

'Quite right, Sergeant. The clients of The Packhorse will be getting tired of us.' He glanced at his watch. 'They may still be there; we'll go and join them. In the meantime, the kiosk will be sealed off till it can be gone over.' He rose, and Jackson with him. 'From now on, Mrs Selby, Constable Frost will keep an eye on you. Just take normal precautions and try not to worry.'

Jessica sat with clenched hands as Matthew saw the policemen out. Try not to worry! Hysterical laughter rose in a tide inside her. Even if she weren't raped or murdered, her marriage was under threat. Matthew wouldn't easily forget her greeting of him. And still the inane rhymes went round and round in her head. *Nobody asked you, sir, she said.*

As Matthew turned from the door she struggled to her feet. 'The beef will be grossly overdone, but we'll have to make the best of it. Will you lay the table?'

Silently, pursuing their own thoughts, they set about preparing for lunch.

It happened about nine-thirty. Lois was relaxing in her room, as she'd been twelve days earlier when Frances came to her door and the whole nightmare began. This time, the interruption was more dramatic. There was a cry, faint through intervening walls, followed by frenzied shouts of 'Help! Help! Someone come quickly!'

Lois wrenched open her door as Pammy Ironside hurried past. 'It's Mrs Southern,' she said over her shoulder. Together they ran into the old lady's room. Immediately opposite, the curtains were pulled aside and the window gaped wide, its sash pushed up to its highest extent. Mrs Southern lay in bed, sheet to her chin, as Pammy had left her twenty minutes earlier.

Lois ran to the window and leant out, listening intently. Immediately to her right, the skeletal framework of the fire escape led down to the dark garden. Nothing moved, either on it or in the shadows beneath, but the lawn had been cut that afternoon, and some wet blades of grass glistened on the broad sill.

Heart pounding, she turned back into the room. Pammy was bending over Mrs Southern.

'What happened?' Lois tried to speak calmly.

The old voice was surprisingly firm. 'I wasn't asleep, thank God. If I had been, I doubt if I'd have woken again.'

'It was only a burglar!' Lois said sharply, but her eyes fell under the scathing glance.

Ignoring her, Mrs Southern continued. 'The window was open a few inches, as I like it. The first sound I heard was it being pushed up. I was more puzzled than afraid. Then the curtain was pulled aside and a foot came over the sill. That's when I screamed. I startled him, of course. He hesitated—perhaps wondering if he'd time to silence me— then, as I went on shouting, he retreated rapidly.'

'Stay here, Nurse,' Lois ordered quickly. 'I'll send some tea up and get on to the police.'

So for the second time that day, Webb and Jackson drove out to Westridge, followed by Scenes of Crime officers. 'At least,' Webb said hopefully, 'we should get a footprint. There was a heavy dew this evening.'

But he was wrong. The fire escape was innocent of any recognizable prints, though a smudged wetness appeared on its steps, accompanied by blades of grass. The explanation was provided by Mrs Southern.

'He was in his stocking feet,' she said positively, in reply to his question. 'Grey socks. I saw them quite clearly.'

'Over his shoes, no doubt,' Webb said disgustedly. 'What else did you see, ma'am?'

'A pair of hands, in gloves, and a—a woolly face, with gaps for eyes.'

'The helmet again. Nothing you could recognize?'

'No. I *think* he wore a black, high-necked sweater, but I couldn't be sure.'

Webb turned to Lois. 'Were the side gates locked, as I requested?'

'I bolted them myself, before it got dark.'

'Then how the hell did he get in?'

When they went downstairs, the Scenes of Crime man told them. The left-hand gate had been unlocked. 'It's easily done, Guv. The bolt's down near the bottom and there's a big enough gap underneath to put your hand through and draw it back.'

Lois said quietly, 'Was it simply a burglar, Chief Inspector?'

'I'm afraid not, Mrs Winter. The woollen helmet's pretty conclusive.'

'That's what I thought. But what's been worrying me is how he knew which was Mrs Southern's room.'

'Unfortunately she received a lot of publicity in the press. The point was made that her window overlooked Hinckley's Cottage.'

'So does my own.'

'But not directly. Our man could have stood on the lower road and picked out the most likely.'

'Will he try again, do you think?'

'No, Mrs Winter, I can reassure you on that at least. There'll be a man in the grounds until this business is sorted out. Two incidents here are more than enough.'

Back in the car, Jackson asked, 'Do you really reckon that, Guv? That the villain sussed out the window from the road?'

'It's feasible.'

'It's also feasible he had inside knowledge.'

'That possibility didn't escape me, Ken. Our friend is certainly stepping up his activities. We can only hope that will prove his undoing.'

CHAPTER 11

It rained all day Tuesday. Matthew had left early for Oxford, and Jessica spent the day at home. She could have phoned The Willows for someone to collect her, but since the incident on Sunday night, it no longer seemed a sanctuary. The frightened faces and hushed voices yesterday had added to her own unease, especially since she felt responsible. If she hadn't followed up the figure with the sack, it would never have happened.

However, Mrs Southern had seemed of all of them the least upset by her adventure. To her, it was the final vindi-cation of her sight of 'Santa Claus', and she savoured it to the full.

So, though it was cowardly to desert her, Jessica'd been glad of the excuse of Matthew's absence. And she'd have Carrie's company during the morning.

In the event, that was a disappointment. Pale and drawn, Carrie crept mouse-like round the house, her red-rimmed eyes slipping away from Jessica's every time they met. What was *wrong* with the girl? she thought irritably. She'd been bright enough when they'd first come, but since the news of Mrs Cowley's murder she'd gone steadily downhill. And today of all days, Jessica needed cheerful companionship.

Thank goodness she'd be out this evening. She liked the Markhams, but she'd gladly have gone anywhere to get away from the cottage and the brooding atmosphere which she now imagined filled it.

This intensified when, having prepared the lunch, Carrie left, since even her wan face provided another human presence in the house. The heavy rain driving against the windows and the lowering sky made the room prematurely dark. Jessica found herself glancing repeatedly at the phone, and praying it wouldn't ring. If it did, should she answer it? She was relieved when it was time to change.

For the first time, she had to manœuvre the stairs alone. Suppose she fell? How long would it be till she was found? And who would find her? The hairs rose in the nape of her neck.

But she didn't fall. The lighter plaster was easier to manipulate, and she reached the landing without mishap and with a sense of triumph which lightened her mood. By the time Charles Palmer called as arranged, she was waiting for him.

He stood at the door under a huge umbrella, the rain slanting down behind him, and her sense of unreality returned. She was setting off in the darkness with a man who might be a murderer. How did she know his wife was waiting in the car?

His bright black eyes were on her face, his dark hair tightly curled in the damp atmosphere. *Curly locks, Curly locks—*

'Give me one of your crutches and take my arm,' he said. Oh God, Matthew, why aren't you here? Fearfully she launched herself on the slippery path, clinging to the wet sleeve of his mackintosh. Behind the streaming car window, the pale disc of his wife's face swam like an exotic fish in a tank. But at least she was there. Jessica shook her head to clear it, and the rain that fell on her face dispelled the fantasy.

'What a night!' Annette Palmer exclaimed, as her husband helped Jessica into the back. Charles shook the umbrella and got into the car, his hair glistening with droplets in the light which, as he slammed the door, went out.

'How's your husband's research coming along?' Annette inquired, as they set off slowly along the dark tunnel of the road.

'He seems quite pleased with it.'

'Will he get it done in time? Though I suppose it won't matter now, if you want to stay longer.'

Jessica repressed a shudder. 'The lease was for four weeks. I think he'll have finished by then.' Blessed, blessed London, with its crowds and streetlights and theatres. How she longed to be back there! Would they be free to return when they wished, or would that hard-eyed detective keep them here till he'd closed the case?

They were turning into the driveway of the Markhams' house. No sign yet of Matthew's car. Guy appeared with another umbrella, and they were shepherded into the warm, welcoming hall. A small boy, in dressing-gown and slippers, watched them shyly from the kitchen door.

'William's just finishing his supper,' Kathy explained. 'I said he could come and say good night before going upstairs. Now, come inside and get warm, everyone. I dare say we don't *need* a fire yet, but it helps to lighten the gloom!'

'Where's Angie?' Jessica asked as she was assisted into the sitting-room.

'Tuesday's her late evening. She stays at school for drama, and doesn't get back till nine. Now, what's everyone drinking?' Kathy paused. 'By the way, I suggest we keep off the topic of rape and murder. For this evening at least, let's enjoy ourselves.'

'Here, here!' Charles said heartily, his back to the fire,

and Jessica settled into her chair with a small sigh of relief. But just once, before she closed her mind to the subject, she let herself cast a considering look at Annette Palmer. With more make-up, Jessica thought professionally, she could be quite attractive. As it was, with her fair hair, pale skin, and the cream silk dress she wore, there was no contrast and the effect was insipid. What, she wondered before she could stop herself, had Freda Cowley looked like? More vibrant, she felt sure.

She took the glass Guy offered her. Kathy was saying, 'It was so sweet of you to have Angie round. She came home positively glowing.'

'She has definite promise,' Jessica said, 'but of course she's very young. She might change her mind about what she wants to do.'

'I doubt it. She's fifteen now, and she's lived and breathed theatre since she was six, and we took her to *Peter Pan*. As far as she's concerned, O- and A-levels are a necessary evil to get through before she can concentrate on acting.'

'Well, if in a few years' time she comes to London, do ask her to contact me. I might be able to help.'

The conversation became general, and turned to the Michaelmas Fair at the end of the week.

'You will be coming, won't you, Jessica?' Kathy asked.

'This Saturday? Unfortunately Matthew has to be in London.'

'Then come with us. Will you be able to walk well enough?'

'As long as I can sit down when I need to.'

'That's no problem. It's usually good fun—the travelling fair comes—and it'll pass the time for you, while Matthew's away.'

Jessica looked again at the clock. She hoped his delayed arrival wasn't holding up the meal. Young William came in to say good night and was packed off to bed. Second drinks were served. Charles launched into an explicit description of a golf tournament he'd just won. And at last, as the hands of the clock reached eight-forty-five, there was a ring at the bell. Guy went to answer it and a minute later Matthew appeared in the doorway, his hair tousled and his trousers caked with mud.

'Apologies, everyone. What a night to have a puncture! I'll clean myself up and be with you in a moment.'

Guy directed him to the cloakroom and had a drink ready for his return. 'Where did it happen?'

'On the A420. I'd been making quite good time until then, and knowing you were waiting made matters worse.' He emptied his glass quickly, and Kathy led the way to the dining-room.

It was probably hindsight that made those next few minutes portentous. At the time, Jessica was aware simply of heightened perception—a smudge of mud on Matthew's cheek which he'd missed when washing, the elaborate embroidery on her napkin, the globules of cream in her soup. Behind her, rain rattled against the windows, and the panes shook in a gust of wind.

'Foretaste of winter,' Guy proclaimed. 'Before we know where we are, it'll be Christmas!'

'Oh no!' Kathy protested. 'This is a freak day—September's my favourite month. Still warm and sunny enough to sit out during the day, but cool in the evening, and when everyone's safely home you can draw the curtains and be cosy.'

'Talking of being safely home,' Guy said, 'shouldn't Angie be back?' As he spoke, they heard the sound of the front door.

'There she is now,' Kathy said. 'She'll have eaten at school, but she'll probably look in to say hello.'

Matthew, across the table from Jessica, had stopped eating and was looking towards the door. When it remained closed, he continued with his soup. Kathy, too, was expecting her daughter to come in.

'Angie?' she called. There was no reply. She frowned. 'That was the front door, wasn't it?'

'I'll go and see.' Guy pushed back his chair and left the room. The rest of them finished their soup and continued talking. After five minutes had elapsed, Kathy, with a murmured apology, also excused herself.

Annette said in a low voice, 'I hope nothing's wrong.'

'She's probably had a row with her boyfriend,' Charles opined, and laughed.

'It's a difficult age,' Annette agreed, talking, Jessica felt, merely to fill in the increasingly surprising absence of their hosts. 'Our son, who's seventeen, is going through a very moody phase, slouching about with a face like thunder and refusing to answer when called. Usually he responds better to Charles than to me, but at the moment he won't go near him. He even—'

'I gave him a good dressing-down,' Charles interrupted. 'He's only sulking.'

Annette shook her head worriedly. 'No, dear, it's more than that. He—'

'Get too big for their boots, kids these days. Think the whole universe should revolve round them. When I was—'

The door opened suddenly and they all turned towards it. Guy stood there, his face white. 'I'm sorry, everyone, I'm afraid we have a crisis on our hands.'

Jessica said quickly, 'Angie?'

He met her eyes. 'She's been raped,' he said flatly. Then as though speaking the word had finally brought home the fact, he repeated, 'Raped!' and his voice broke.

Matthew and Charles came simultaneously to their feet and everyone exclaimed at once. Guy held up a hand. 'I've phoned the police, and we have to take her there at once; apparently time is of the essence. We're leaving now. Kathy says please will you stay and finish the meal—it's all in the oven.'

'But you don't want us here!' Jessica cried, and again Guy raised his hand.

'On the contrary, we do. William's asleep upstairs: he can't be left, and we don't want to wake him to this. Anyway there's no point in wasting good food.' He tried to smile. 'Seriously, we'd be enormously grateful if you'd stay till we get back.'

'Guy!' Kathy's voice sounded shrilly from the hall.

'I'm coming. Please!' he said to his guests. Then the dining-room door closed, and a moment later the front door too.

'Oh God!' Annette said on a high note. 'Where's this going to end?'

While the examination and tests were being conducted, the Markhams tried to answer Webb's questions.

'Your daughter will be making a statement to the woman police officer,' he said, 'but she must have talked to you on the way here. Please tell me everything she said.' He paused. 'I know how difficult this is for you, but it's possible she might omit something important from her official account, either from forgetfulness or because she's too embarrassed to repeat it. Will you tell me, Mr Markham, exactly what happened when you left your guests to go and find her?'

'She was in her room,' Guy said. 'Lying fully dressed across her bed, face down. She was soaking wet and covered in mud, just like—' He broke off.

'Just like what?'

Guy raised his haggard face. 'I was going to say, just like Matthew Selby. He'd arrived twenty minutes earlier, also wet and muddy.'

'He didn't come with his wife?'

'No. He'd told us he'd be late, so the Palmers brought her.'

'And how did Mr Selby explain his condition?'

'He said he'd had a puncture, on the way back from Oxford. My God, you don't think—?'

'Go on with your account, please.'

'Well, she was shaking. I thought she was crying, but she wasn't. When I went round the bed, I saw her eyes were open, just staring straight ahead. And this convulsive trembling, making her teeth chatter. I think I knew, then. It's what we've been dreading for the last fortnight.'

'What did she tell you?'

'She caught the usual bus home after drama. Holly Beck, who normally travels with her, was off with 'flu and there was no one she knew on the bus. She was almost the last to get off, at Green Lane.'

'How far is that from your house?'

'A couple of hundred yards. It was raining hard, and she hadn't an umbrella. She was pulling up the hood of her mac, when, as she put it, something got in the way. At the same time she felt a prick on her neck, and this voice said in her ear, "*One for the little girl who lives down the lane.*" God!' Guy exploded, clenching his hands. 'If I ever catch up with the bastard—'

Kathy reached out, closing her hand over his. After a moment he went on expressionlessly, 'He took her to the pub garden—The Packhorse. Every now and then, as the door swung open, she could hear voices and laughter, but she had that goddamned woollen thing over her head, and couldn't see a thing. Then he—he made her say nursery rhymes. She was crying so much she could hardly speak, but he wouldn't let her stop. Her mind went blank, she said, and he kept prompting her. God, I can't believe this. Is it really happening?'

He drew a deep breath, and added more calmly, 'I'm sorry, Chief Inspector.'

'How exactly did he prompt her, Mr Markham?'

'He said, "Start with *Ride a cock horse,*" and when she came to an end, he asked for *Polly Flinders*. But he was *hurting* her, for Christ sake! God, it's bad enough when he attacks women, but a young girl—' He stopped again and dashed his hand across his eyes. Beside him, Kathy had started to weep softly.

Webb went across to his cupboard, took out a bottle of brandy and two glasses. There were times when his job sickened him. God grant that the girl hadn't conceived, like Carrie Speight. He handed her parents a glass each.

'Don't worry about driving home, we'll take you back in a police car. If time hadn't been so vital, we'd have sent one to collect you. Now, is there any chance she recognized the voice?'

Guy shook his head. 'He spoke in whispers, apparently.'

'And when it was over?'

'He tipped her on to her face, threatened her if she tried to look at him, and untied her hands. Then he pulled off the helmet and left her lying there.' He paused. 'Now that we're here, Chief Inspector, there's something else. God knows I don't like pointing the finger, but now Angie's involved—'

'Yes?'

'It was something she said yesterday, when we were having supper. We were discussing tonight's dinner party, and young Charlie Palmer's name came up. Angie suddenly said she'd seen him on the day of the murder. At Freda's house.'

'*What?*'

'That was my reaction.' A tap on the door interrupted him and Sally Pierce came in with Angie. The girl was quite composed. Kathy got up quickly and went to her, putting an arm round her. Webb rose to his feet.

'All right, Miss Markham? Come and sit down for a moment, will you.' He smiled at the girl, leading her to a chair, and even in her distress, Kathy was surprised how it transformed his face. He's quite attractive, she thought in surprise.

'Your father was saying you saw young Palmer at Mrs Cowley's.'

Angie sent Markham a look of reproach. 'It was in the morning.'

'Even so, we need to know of anyone who called. How did you happen to see him?'

'I was cycling past on the way to the tennis club, about

eleven, I suppose. I just glanced up the path and he was standing at the door.'

'He didn't see you?'

'I don't think so. I didn't call to him because I had a court booked and I was late.' She hesitated. 'I'm sorry if I should have told you, but since Auntie Freda was alive at lunch-time, I didn't think it was important.'

'Was she talking to him?'

'No, the door was closed. She might not even have been home.'

'In which case,' Webb said quietly, 'he could have called back later.'

Her eyes widened and he said more gently still, 'Miss Markham, I don't want to upset you, but could it have been Charlie Palmer who attacked you tonight?'

She caught her breath. 'Charlie wouldn't—I mean—' She paused, steadied herself. 'I don't *think* so. He seemed —older, somehow.'

'Thank you. There's no need to keep you any longer. A car is waiting downstairs and an officer will follow behind in your own car. Thank you all for your help.'

When, eventually, the ghastly evening was over and the Palmers were preparing for bed, Annette said suddenly, 'You don't think Matthew Selby had anything to do with it, do you?'

Charles paused in the act of unbuttoning his shirt. 'The thought had crossed my mind.'

'But surely he wouldn't risk it, when he was on the way there himself?'

'I shouldn't think so, since he'd know Angie would arrive soon after in the same condition. No doubt the police will check the timings.'

'And the puncture story.' Annette brushed her pale, fluffy hair thoughtfully. 'I shouldn't like to be in the Selbys' shoes. Before they came, this was a quiet, peaceful village, and look at it now.'

Charles reached for his pyjamas. 'Remember Kathy saying there'd be no talk of rape or murder this evening? How's that for irony?'

Annette shivered. 'For the first time in my life, I'm glad I haven't a daughter.'

Down on the lower road, the Selbys were also discussing the evening.

'I'll remember that meal for the rest of my life,' Jessica said, 'every mouthful of it. It was like being on stage and having to finish the act, though the producer and the audience had gone home.'

'The *Mary Celeste* in reverse.' Matthew gave a brief laugh. 'You know, if I were trying, I don't think I could arouse friend Webb's suspicions more than I am doing. He'll be round first thing, mark my words, examining my tyres with more than cursory interest.'

'Darling—'

'What?'

'Nothing. Just try not to antagonize him.'

He leant over, kissed her, and switched out the light. ''Night, my sweet. Tomorrow is another day, thank God.'

But Jessica lay staring at the ceiling, remembering his odd moment of tension when Angie arrived home. Had anyone else noticed it? And what had occasioned it? A flashback to the embarrassment of his original meeting with her? Or was he merely waiting to greet his hosts' daughter? It was a question that would have to go unanswered. After Sunday, any further probing could damage their marriage irreparably.

With a small sigh, she settled herself to sleep.

'I've got that info you wanted, Guv,' Jackson said. 'Young Palmer goes to Greystones College, in Oxbury.'

'Thanks, Ken. We'll be waiting outside about four; he's likely to talk more freely away from home.' Webb pushed his drawer shut and got to his feet. 'Well, back we go to

Westridge. We should take lodgings there.'

'To look at Selby's car?'

'Got it in one. That rain last night'll have done nothing for Dick Hodges. He's out at The Packhorse now.'

They stopped at the pub on their way through the village, but nothing of note had been found. Nor were they any more unfortunate at Hinckley's. Selby met them at the door with a sour smile.

'I was expecting you, Chief Inspector. I thought you'd want to see the wheel before I took it to the garage.'

'Good of you.'

As he might have known, there was no doubt about the puncture. It was proving a decidedly unfruitful day, and by the time they drew up at Greystones College, he had had enough of it. Nevertheless, as the first pupils began to come out of the gates in their blue and white striped blazers, he resignedly got out of the car and stood waiting with Jackson.

'There he is!' he said suddenly. 'Bring him over, Ken.'

Charles Palmer junior looked uncannily like his father, the same dark crinkly hair, florid colouring and bold black eyes. Webb watched while Jackson discreetly detached him from his friends, then went to meet them.

''Afternoon, sir,' he said blandly, suppressing a smile as Charlie's apprehension visibly lessened at the form of address. 'Like a word, if we may. We won't keep you long. Let's take a stroll by the river.'

Charlie shot him a questioning look, but fell into step meekly enough between the detectives.

'Now, Mr Palmer,' Webb began, as they followed the path leading down to the water, 'you knew Mrs Cowley, I believe?'

Charlie's pink tongue flicked out and moistened his lips. 'Yes.'

'How well?'

'Only casually. She lived at the other end of the village.'

Webb changed his tactics abruptly. 'Get on well with your dad, do you?'

Taken off guard, Charlie flushed a dark red. 'All right,' he said gruffly.

'That's not what I heard.' A shot in the dark, that. He hadn't heard anything.

There was a pause. 'Well, he gets on my back sometimes. I reckon all fathers do.'

'You don't see eye to eye about things?'

'Not always.'

'About Mrs Cowley, for instance?' Another blind stab, but again it struck home. The boy's high colour ebbed away, leaving his face blotchy.

'I don't know what you mean.'

'Mr Palmer, you were seen calling at Hinckley's Cottage on the day Mrs Cowley died.'

The boy stopped abruptly, and the policemen with him. Beside them, the river Kittle slurped against its banks with a gentle slapping sound.

'We understand,' Webb continued, 'that she had one or two gentlemen friends. I take it you weren't among them?'

His irony was wasted on Charlie. He said in a high voice, 'I told you, I hardly knew her.'

'Then why did you call on her?'

A moorhen had come into sight, paddling gently down the centre of the water.

'I'm waiting, Mr Palmer.'

The boy said in a rush, 'To tell her to keep her hands off my father.'

'Ah.' Over his bowed head, Webb's eyes met Jackson's. 'And did you?'

He nodded miserably.

'What did she say?'

'Told me not to meddle in things that don't concern me.' He raised his head defiantly. 'But it *does* concern me. I love my mum, and—' He broke off, then said slowly, 'You don't think I *killed* her, do you?'

'No, I don't think that. But you should have volunteered

this information, you know. You could have been the last person to see her.'

'But she had lunch with Mr Selby at The Orange Tree. Everyone knows that.'

'Does your father know you went to see her?'

'No.'

'Does he realize you know of his association with her?'

'Yes. He was phoning her one afternoon. He didn't know I was home.'

'How did he react?'

'He tried blustering, but I told him I wasn't a kid. Anyone who phoned Mrs Cowley was after the same thing. So then he tried the man-to-man scene, about no one being hurt by it. He made me *sick*!'

Webb stared after the moorhen. 'What time did you arrive at Hinckley's?'

'Mid-morning sometime.'

'And left?'

'I was only there five minutes. I could have saved my breath.'

Webb sighed. 'Was your father at home that evening?'

'Yes. He did his best to talk me round, but I wouldn't speak to him. I haven't spoken to him properly since.'

A bus rumbled along the road at the top of the path. 'Should you have been on that?' Charlie nodded. 'We'll give you a lift back.'

They drove in silence out of the little town and on to the main road to Heatherton. As they reached the turn-off for Westridge, the boy said suddenly, 'I suppose Mum *is* tired a lot of the time.'

'Quite,' said Webb.

It was with relief that the three of them parted company at the Green Lane bus stop. Webb watched the boy walk towards his home. 'Poor little devil,' he said. 'Well, Ken, I reckon we'll call it a day. Better luck tomorrow, maybe.'

CHAPTER 12

Webb had just arrived home when Hannah called. They'd not seen each other in the last twelve days. She had decided, in view of Susan's proximity, to leave the first move to him, and he had not made it. He'd had little time for personal problems, and in any case was too unsettled by his ambiguous reaction to Susan voluntarily to seek out either of them.

During the summer, he'd feared Hannah might meet someone in Europe who'd take his place. Uncomfortably, he accepted she had the same feelings now, but mixed with his guilt was resentment. Damn it, he hadn't *wanted* this to happen. Hannah offered all that he needed, physically, mentally and spiritually, though this last was not a word he was comfortable with. Yet he was susceptible to Susan as to no one else, and until he'd worked her out of his system, by whatever means, her shadow fell across them.

All this jumbled in his mind as he faced Hannah, inhibiting him from doing what he most wanted, which was to take her in his arms.

She said quietly, 'You look tired.'

'I am, yes.' He stood aside. 'Come in.'

'I don't want to add to your problems, but I have to speak to you.'

Oh God, he thought involuntarily, not about Susan!

Having seated herself in her usual chair, Hannah looked up at him. 'David, I don't know whether you realize, but Angie Markham is one of my pupils.'

'My God,' he said flatly. 'No, I didn't.' He poured her a drink and handed it to her.

'Is she all right?'

'You know what happened?' She nodded. 'Well, in the accepted phrase, she's as well as can be expected. I'm not qualified to hold forth on psychological damage, but she has a loving family to support her.'

'Her mother phoned this morning. I just couldn't believe it.' Hannah looked down at her tightly laced hands. 'You mentioned a rape last time I saw you. Are they both connected with the murder?'

'Almost definitely.'

'Then,' she said with bitterness, 'perhaps Angie's lucky; at least she's still alive.' She looked up at him, her tawny hair falling back from her face and exposing her wide brow. 'Why do you suppose he murdered one woman and only raped the other two?'

The other four, Webb thought, but he didn't correct her. 'I don't know. Nor do we know if he raped the murder victim; it was too late to tell.'

She shivered, reached for her drink and took a sip. 'Have you any leads?'

'Nothing significant yet.'

'Then there could be more attacks.'

He didn't reply. Hannah finished her drink quickly and rose to her feet. 'I mustn't take up your time. Thanks for the drink.'

He said impulsively, 'Hannah—' and stopped.

She met his eyes squarely. 'Susan?'

Miserably, he nodded.

'You've seen her again?'

'We had a drink together.'

Any other woman would have persisted: was he still in love with his ex-wife? What about herself? Hannah merely nodded gravely and moved towards the door. He put a hand on her arm.

'Give me time, love. I don't know where the hell I am at the moment.'

'Of course, I'm not—I just wanted to ask about Angie.'

Hannah returned thoughtfully to her own flat. The previous evening, she and Gwen had had one of their rare personal exchanges, and she reflected ruefully that her friend had been right.

Gwen Rutherford, Head Mistress of Ashbourne School for Girls, was a tall woman, gauche in her movements, whose soft hair persistently escaped the confines of its French pleat and whose brown eyes were diffident and apologetic. Yet it was unwise, on this account, to underrate her, for behind that gentle exterior dwelt an iron-willed intellectual, who had long since determined the goals to aim for, and whom nothing would deter from achieving them.

She and Hannah had been friends for years; yet there was in each of them a reserve which precluded the intimate discussions in which other women indulged. All Gwen knew of David was his first name and the fact that he was divorced. She had no inkling that he was the tall, loose-limbed police officer to whom, over two years ago, she had herself introduced Hannah, during an outbreak of anonymous letters at the school.

None the less, awareness of Hannah's abstraction had, the night before, overcome her reticence and, when the drama students had gone and they were sitting over coffee, she said gently, 'Something's wrong, Hannah. Anything I can help with?'

Hannah glanced at her in surprise and shook her head.

'It can be useful, sometimes, to talk things over, but of course I've no wish to pry.'

Hannah stirred her coffee in silence. Then, reaching a decision, she said, 'You know David's been married?'

'I think you mentioned it.'

'His wife's come back.'

'To him?'

'To Shillingham. But he's seen her.'

'And you're jealous?' Gwen's smile took the sting out of the query.

'I think I must be. Isn't that awful?'

'I'd say it was natural. But would you marry him yourself, if he asked you?'

'He won't. Even before this, he wouldn't have.'

'But if he did?'

Hannah shook her head slowly.

'Why not?'

'I'm a career woman, Gwen. You know that.'

'But your careers don't conflict at the moment. Why should they be an obstacle to marriage?'

'It's not only that. We don't—stifle each other by being there all the time, and we're free to—' She broke off with a rueful grimace at her friend's expression.

'—to see other people. Which is just what David's doing.'

'I know it's selfish. I don't want to marry him, but nor do I want anyone else to.'

'This woman already has. It didn't work, so why should they risk it again?'

'David's a complex character. He can be gentle as well as ruthless, and naive as well as astute. Because he once loved her, she still has a hold on him. A lot will depend on whether she wants him back. And why come to Broadshire unless she does?'

'How would you feel if they remarried?'

'Wretched,' Hannah said frankly. 'I want things to go on as they were, which is childish, I know. Nothing lasts for ever.'

She had thought, as she spoke, that seeing him again would give some clue to his feelings. It hadn't. He'd been embarrassed to see her, and that had hurt. If she hadn't genuinely wanted to hear about Angie, she'd have gone straight back downstairs. Yet it was less than a fortnight since they'd made love.

Closing her mind to the memory, Hannah seated herself at the bureau and opened her briefcase. Tomorrow, she'd go to see Angie. The girl would be better at school than moping under her mother's anxious eyes, and with O-levels looming, she couldn't afford to miss lessons. As for David Webb, she thought with a flash of rebellion, he could sort out his own problems. She had better things to do.

Uncapping her pen, she drew a sheaf of papers towards her.

On the floor above, Webb's reflections were no more comfortable. He knew the rape had been only part of the reason for Hannah's visit as, two weeks before, the earlier one had been for Susan's. He loathed rape, was shamed by it on behalf of his sex, and felt inhibited when discussing it with women, not least those whose own bodies he had known.

And he was surrounded by women, he thought irritably, running a hand through his hair. Not only Hannah and Susan, but Angie and Frances Daly and Carrie Speight. Not to mention Freda Cowley. All of them, even poor, dead Freda, seemed to be mutely appealing to him to avenge them. And he didn't know what to do next.

Tired and dispirited, he considered taking out his sketch-pad and, by filling it with caricatures of the protagonists, see if, as so often in the past, they would point him to the murderer.

But he wasn't in the mood. Instead, he refilled his glass, switched on the television, and went to see what was in the larder.

Nor was PC Frost any happier. He sat glumly at his supper table, the heavy body of the dog across his feet, and even the smell of Margie's suet dumplings failed to cheer him. He watched as she poured hot syrup over them and slid the plate towards him. Across the table, his son Benjie munched appreciatively, his full mouth not inhibiting him from retailing the day's news.

'The old man had to get the vet in to old Daisy. She was taking her time calving, and no wonder, since it was a breech.'

'Not at the table, love,' admonished his mother automatically.

'Bob was up with her all night,' Benjie continued, as

though she hadn't spoken. 'He looked fair shattered, though whether it was lack of sleep or fretting over his young lady, I couldn't say.'

'Della Speight, that'll be,' Margie remarked, and in subconscious association patted her hair.

'Aye. In a fair tither that the rapist will get her, like he got her sister.'

'Watch your tongue, lad,' Ted said sharply. 'No names in rape cases. You know that.'

'Oh come on, Dad, the whole village knows. Bob keeps asking if you're near to getting your hands on him.'

Ted chewed solidly, glad of the excuse not to reply. What had come over the place? Only a few weeks back, things were the same as always. Now, every newspaper had Westridge splashed over its front page and he was deeply mortified.

'And now the Markham kid,' Benjie continued, his father's depression affecting him, too. 'Young girl like that. He wants flogging, if you ask me.' He glanced shrewdly at Ted. 'Any ideas, Dad? Off the record, like?'

'Father's doing what he can,' Margie said comfortably before he could reply. 'And with Mr Webb helping him, they'll sort it out soon enough. Eat up, now. More dumplings, anyone?'

'You have an admirer, darling!' Matthew said lightly when he brought in Jessica's breakfast. 'An offering was left on the doorstep with the milk.'

'What is it?'

'I've no idea, but there's a heart on the box. I hadn't room on the tray, or I'd have brought it up.'

'How intriguing. Do get it, darling.'

He returned with a white confectioner's box tied with red ribbon. On the top, a heart had been drawn with a red felt pen.

Jessica pulled off the ribbon and lifted the lid. 'How very odd,' she said after a moment.

'What is it?' Coffee-pot in hand, Matthew moved round

the bed. Inside the box, in two neat rows, nestled a dozen jam tarts. 'Good God! Is there a card with them?'

'Not unless it's underneath.' Carefully, Jessica lifted each tart in turn, but the box contained nothing else.

'Valentine's Day in September. I'd plumped for Leo as the most likely donor, but jam tarts are hardly his line.'

'Well,' Jessica said, closing the lid, 'it makes a change from chocolates. They look good, too. We'll have them for tea.'

'Oh, Miss James! How kind! Do come in.'

Side-stepping the bucket of water in the porch, Hannah went into the hall. Kathy threw it a distracted glance. 'That must be my son's. He brought some tadpoles home from school.' She showed Hannah into the sitting-room. 'Just one moment, I'll ask Carrie to bring coffee.'

'How's Angie, Mrs Markham?'

'She seems all right.' She hesitated. 'We were wondering about school. What do you think?'

'I feel it would be good for her to come back.'

'That's what my husband said, but you know how cruel children can be.'

'I think we can forestall that. Either Miss Rutherford or I will speak to the girls.'

A pale young woman came in with a tray of coffee, put it on the table, and left the room.

'Where's Angie now?' Hannah asked.

'In her room, playing records.'

'May she join us?'

'Of course. I'll bring another cup.'

To Hannah's relief, Angie looked no different from at Tuesday's drama class. Though initially embarrassed, Hannah's natural manner and the general conversation reassured her, and she relaxed.

'I hope you've not forgotten the hockey match,' Hannah said casually. 'We'll need you, against St Anne's.'

The girl flashed a quick look at her mother, and Hannah

saw Mrs Markham give an encouraging nod.

'I—I'll be back tomorrow.'

'That's fine.'

Angie paused, then leant forward excitedly. 'Miss James, did you know Jessica Randal's staying in the village? I went round there last Saturday, and we read through a scene of her new play.'

'How exciting! Was she impressed?'

'Yes. She promised to send us tickets, and she told Mummy if I keep on with my acting, I can look her up in London, and she'll try to help.'

'Then you're a very lucky girl. No matter how much talent you have, a friend at court is invaluable.'

The doorbell rang, and the woman who'd brought the coffee went to open it. A minute later, Hannah looked up to see David and another man standing in the doorway. She rose to her feet as Mrs Markham went to greet him.

'Chief Inspector, this is Miss James, Deputy Head of Angie's school, who's kindly come to see her. Chief Inspector Webb, Miss James, and—?'

'Sergeant Jackson,' David said. His eyes held Hannah's. 'Good morning, Miss James.'

'Good morning.' She turned to Angie, whose apprehension had returned with the arrival of the police. 'I'll tell Miss Bates you'll be back for the match. Thanks for the coffee, Mrs Markham.'

Kathy went with her to the door. 'I'm so sorry—I suppose the police—'

'Don't worry, I've accomplished what I came for.' Avoiding the bucket again, Hannah walked down the path.

On their way back to the station, Jackson said suddenly, 'I may be imagining things, but I'd like to ring round and see if anyone else found something odd when they woke up this morning.'

'What do you mean, odd?'

'Like that pail of water at the Markhams'.'

'But it was the boy's. Mrs Markham explained as we left.'

'That's what she assumed, but I had a quick look and there were no tadpoles. And remember when we called at The Willows? There was that broken egg on the path, just inside the gate.'

'So what? Some kid had probably balanced it on the wall. What are you getting at, Ken?'

'*Humpty Dumpty had a great fall?* And Jack and Jill's pail of water? Perhaps this thing's getting to me, but—'

Webb whistled softly. 'You could be on to something. I didn't see the significance, but you're more geared to nursery rhymes. Right; ring round by all means. I don't know where it'll get us, but it'll be interesting to see what turns up.'

Webb reported on Jackson's findings later that afternoon when, at Chief Superintendent Fleming's request, he called in at Headquarters.

'And the upshot was that the Selbys had received some jam tarts with a heart on the box; the Palmers, who have an ornamental well in the garden, found a toy cat floating in it; Carrie Speight reported a wreath of roses on the step with a handkerchief tied to it, and at Sandon Hall a walnut tree was decorated with a pear and nutmeg covered in foil.'

Fleming frowned, tapping his pen on his thumbnail. 'I don't like it, Spider. We're getting enough stick from the public, with two weeks gone and no arrest imminent, without the murderer himself playing silly buggers with us.'

'If he was doing, sir.'

Fleming's frown deepened. 'Explain.'

'Well, sir, firstly we don't *know* it was the murderer, though I admit it seems likely.'

'Who the hell else? Willie Winkie on his run through the town?'

Webb allowed himself a politic smile. 'But if it *was* Chummie, then I don't think he was playing games. Or only of the cat and mouse variety.'

'You mean these objects were meant as a warning?'

'I'd say so. He's already tangled with most of the recipients.' He paused. 'There's something else bothering me, sir. As far as we can establish, our man has raped before—the woman in Ashmartin, if no one else. But why the three-year gap? Then for some reason he *kills* his victim, after which he reverts to rape again. It's not consistent.'

'Go on.'

'Once a man's killed for sex, rape alone doesn't satisfy him.'

'You're not suggesting at this stage that we've *two* villains at large?'

'No, there aren't likely to be two nursery-rhyme freaks.'

'Unless one copied the other.'

'But there'd been no publicity about the rhymes till the body was found, and Mrs Cowley was killed *between* the attacks on the Ashmartin woman and Mrs Daly. Yet both of them were forced to recite rhymes, and the deceased had one in her pocket. What I'm getting at is this: we've no evidence that Mrs Cowley *was* raped.'

'Only because of advanced decomposition.'

'But suppose she hadn't been, that she was killed for an entirely different reason.'

'Like what?'

Webb shrugged. 'One of the standard motives: fear, gain, blackmail.'

'But if he hadn't raped her, why draw attention to himself by putting the rhyme in her pocket?'

'That's a hard one. Perhaps as a challenge, or perhaps because he gets such a kick out of them that he couldn't help himself. He had to leave his trademark.'

Fleming considered that. Then he said, 'So what do you propose?'

'We'll go through the statements from a different angle. See if anyone had anything to gain by her death, or a secret she might have stumbled on.'

'There were quite a few cheating on their wives and open to blackmail.'

'It would have to be more than that.'

'Suppose one had a rich wife and didn't want to lose out through divorce?'

'I doubt if there's that kind of money in Westridge, apart from the Sandons.'

'Then what about them? The goofy one, who wanders the woods spouting poetry? Or the three sons sowing their wild oats?'

Webb said slowly, 'The Honourable Leo's a non-secretor. It's possible. There's been scandal a-plenty over the years, we might be due for some more.' He stretched, easing his aching back. 'In the meantime we'll do the best we can with the latest exhibits. I doubt if we'll get much from the toy cat. It's old, only one eye and an ear missing, though we can check with the manufacturers who stocked it and when. Davis and Trent are covering the florists, but the tarts looked homemade, Mrs Selby said, and she's eaten them.'

Fleming sighed. 'OK, Spider, keep me posted. And for God's sake nab him soon.'

'I'll do my best, sir,' Webb replied.

In his basement sitting-room at The Willows, Frank Chitty sat in his rocking-chair whittling wood and humming softly to himself. Under his skilled fingers, the wafer-thin shavings fluttered to the ground like curly cream snowflakes as the wood took shape. A busby, a round head and square shoulders, legs standing to attention. There were five companions awaiting this toy soldier, ready painted and varnished and lined up neatly in the box under his bed. Six was enough, he reckoned. He'd go back to dolls next. Dolls was his favourite, Dutch dolls, they called 'em, with their painted black hair and the red circles on their cheeks.

He'd best tidy up before Cook finished in the kitchen. Even in his mind, he no longer used his wife's name. She'd been Cook to him as to everyone else for the last thirty years. Well, he couldn't call her 'Mother', more's the pity, since they'd never had kids. The wooden trains and wagons he'd fashioned so lovingly over the years had no eager recipients in view. Every now and then, when they were taking up too much room, Cook collected them and took them to the kids' hospital. Fair enough. In the early days she'd suggested selling them, but that had upset him. He loved his little wooden figures, and to part with them for money would be like selling children.

Children. He ached for them sometimes. And grand-children he could dandle on his knee and tell fairy stories. And nursery rhymes.

A quiver ran through him and the knife slipped, leaving a bright blood-bead on his finger. *Who killed Cock Robin?* Only it wasn't Cock Robin, but Mrs Cowley down at Hinck-ley's, her with her long legs which she displayed all anyhow getting in and out of her car, and not minding who saw them, either. She'd seen him watching her once, outside the post office, and laughed at him with her red mouth and bold eyes. He'd dreamt of her once or twice after that, waking trembling and hot with excited shame. Still, a man was a man, and it was a long time since Cook had condoned any hanky-panky, as she called it.

There'd been other things he'd done, too, that he didn't like to think about afterwards.

He wiped the sweat off his forehead with the back of his hand, and, as the shaking lessened, picked up the knife again and went on whittling.

Jessica lay in the dark, listening to Matthew's quiet breath-ing beside her. Her mind was a churning pool in which thoughts darted among the shadows, elusive as fish. Those jam tarts. She'd been appalled, this evening, to learn of their origin. The knowledge that she'd so trustingly eaten them made her stomach heave. Suppose they'd been poisoned? In this menacing world she inhabited, they could easily have been.

Other people had received things, too, the sergeant said on the phone, though he hadn't mentioned who or what.

The Knave of Hearts he stole those tarts and took them clean away. Her hands clenched under the bedclothes. *Stop it!* But God, she was supposed to have police protection, wasn't she, after Sunday's phone-call? Where'd he been, she'd like to know, when the potential murderer crept up to her door? And what was the meaning of these sinister offerings?

She had met Freda Cowley's killer. The thought, hidden in her subconscious since the weekend, emerged clearly for the first time, and she gasped. He had phoned her, personally, and had stood on the step below this very window as she and Matthew lay sleeping. Suppose he'd climbed up the ivy and into the window, as he'd tried to enter Mrs Southern's?

Rigid with fear, Jessica remembered that the window was open now. Suppose he came back tonight? Under the thin cotton nightdress her body was bathed in sweat. She couldn't get out of bed without disturbing Matthew, but she wouldn't close her eyes as long as that window remained open. Tentatively she touched his arm.

'Matthew—'

He sighed, stirred, and settled back again.

'Darling.' She gave his arm a little shake.

'Um? What is it?'

'I know I'm being silly, but would you close the window, please?'

He reached for the light switch and in the sudden brilliance stared down at her. 'You woke me to ask me that?' Then, seeing the hair clinging wetly to her face, he realized her fear.

'All right.' He swung his legs out of bed. 'But remember to shut it on Saturday, because I shan't be here to do it for you.'

In five minutes he was asleep again, but for Jessica, with the spectre of Saturday added to her fears, it was a full hour before she slid uneasily into oblivion.

CHAPTER 13

Before she went to The Willows the next morning, Jessica sought out Carrie in the kitchen.

'I've a favour to ask you,' she said with a smile. 'My husband has to go to London tomorrow, and he'll be away overnight. Could you possibly come and sleep here? At the moment I don't want to be alone.'

Carrie turned from the sink. 'Oh Mrs Selby, I'm so sorry. I'd have been glad to, but I promised to babysit for Mrs Plunkett. They're going to a dance in Shillingham and won't be back till late, so she asked me to stay the night.'

It hadn't occurred to Jessica that her request might be declined. She was tempted to plead, but Carrie was unlikely to go back on her word, and a second refusal would be belittling. She could only accept her repeated apology and leave the room.

She reported the outcome to Matthew in the car. 'It was rather a blow. I was counting on her.'

'It can't be helped, and you'll be just as safe without her. She'd have been company, but she's not an armed guard. Anyway, it's only for one night and you'll have spent the afternoon at the Fair. You'll probably be glad to relax and have an early night.'

Jessica was unconvinced. She could book into The Orange Tree, but the landlord was already curious about Matthew, and moving out of her own home would draw attention to her fear. If Matthew were going anywhere but to his own family, she'd have gone with him.

'You'll be all right, love,' he added bracingly. 'Don't let it upset you.'

But would this murderer, who knew her, also know Matthew would be away that night?

He drew up outside The Willows and helped her out of the car. 'All right?'

She nodded, smiled and went inside. He stood for a moment looking after her. She was certainly nervous, poor love. He'd been on the point of asking if she could stay at the Hall, when he learned Dominic and Giselle wouldn't be there. As soon as the Fair was over, they were taking his mother to a relative's for a few days, and Matthew knew Jessica would prefer her own company to Leo's.

With a sigh, he got back into the car. It was a nuisance, but he couldn't disappoint Claire by not going to her party. Things would sort themselves out.

The room was silent except for her sobbing. He stood at the window, moodily staring out at the dull afternoon. At last he said angrily, 'Don't you love me any more? Is that it?'

'Of course I love you,' she answered despairingly. 'Do you think I'd go through all this, if I didn't?'

'Well, carrying on like that's not going to change anything.'

'I never thought it would come to this. I've tried to understand, you know I have. You said you were grateful.'

'It's not as if I can help it.'

She raised her ravaged face. 'But you *can*, love. That part, anyway. We've kept it in check for years now, as long as you—'

'—keep taking the tablets!' he broke in angrily. 'Yes, well, I got tired of that, didn't I? How would you like to spend four days a month doped to the eyeballs?'

Her lips quivered. 'I thought you *wanted* me to help you.' She started to weep again in a series of gulping little moans. 'I couldn't believe it was you. Not this time.'

'Then you were wrong, weren't you? And there's not a thing you can do about it. You're my wife, you can't testify against me.'

'You think I want to?'

'What do you want, then?' She shook her head hopelessly and his face softened. 'Come here.'

Obediently she went to him and his arms closed round her, rocking her as though she were a baby. 'There, there. I'll be a good boy.'

'You'll go back on the pills?'

'I suppose so. Now, dry your eyes and I'll put the kettle on.'

'I made some jam tarts, but—'

'There are biscuits in the tin. They'll be fine.'

She moved away from him, wiping her eyes. Perhaps, if he'd really try again, it might still be all right.

Webb signed off early that evening and went home. The florists had drawn a blank, and the toy firm that manufactured the cat had closed down six years ago. This man had the devil's own luck. He felt tired and stale. Usually after this time on a case, things were falling into place. Now, he felt no further on than when he'd started. *Round and round the garden*—

He let himself into his flat, and as usual stood for some minutes staring down the hill towards Shillingham. Was Hannah back from school yet? Uneasily, he wondered if the underlying distraction of his personal problems was inhibiting his thinking. Yet he could see no avenue he'd not explored. Turning from the window, he set up his easel with none of his usual anticipation. Far from longing to start on the drawing, it was just one more routine to be followed through.

For an hour he sketched continuously, peopling the sheet with the inhabitants of Westridge: Matthew Selby, still his favourite for the part, with an exaggeratedly high forehead and hollow cheeks; his wide-eyed wife, the Speight sisters, Angie Markham. Some overlooked fact about any of them could point him in the right direction.

The doorbell rang suddenly through the flat, and he swore, looking at his watch. Nearly six-thirty. Resignedly he went and opened the door. Susan stood there, her eyes expectantly on his face.

'Hello, Dave.'

The memory of their parting flared between them, the surge of passion which had shaken them both.

'Who gave you my address?'

She smiled. 'You're not the only detective round here.' She studied his face. 'I reckoned it would be harder for you to walk out on me, from your own flat.'

His stomach tightened. He said curtly, 'I'm busy, Susan.'

'Then you'll need someone to cook supper.' She held up a carrier bag. 'Don't mind me, just get on with your work.'

She stepped past him into the minute hall. 'Where's the kitchen? In here?' She opened the door on her left, nodded with satisfaction and went in. Webb closed the outer door and went back to his easel. He continued working for some minutes until her voice disturbed him.

'Sorry, but I can't find the tin-opener.'

He didn't turn. 'There isn't one.'

'That's bloody silly, isn't it?'

'It's deliberate. It would have provided a soft option.'

'Then how do I open the tomato purée? With my teeth?'

'I'm sorry,' he said, opting out of her problems. Grimly he went on sketching, but his concentration was gone. He needed to channel it to such a degree that he could almost step inside the figures on the sheet, imagining their thoughts and smelling their fear. Now, Susan filled his mind, moving about in his kitchen as she had during eleven years of marriage, her scent clinging to edges of the room.

'I wouldn't mind a drink!' she called.

He got to his feet, poured a large one for each of them. He took hers through to the kitchen, watching in silence as she sliced mushrooms. She'd cut a jagged hole in the purée tin, bending a knife in the process.

'It's kidneys Turbigo,' she said. 'Used to be one of your favourites. What do you live on now, without a tin-opener?'

'I survive.' He was acutely aware of her in the small room.

With a conscious effort he left her and returned yet again to his work. Leo Sandon, whom Ken pronounced nutty as a fruit-cake. Was he dangerous? What of Mr Nice Guy Markham? He smiled wryly at the pun before discarding it. Markham's daughter ruled that out.

Behind him, Susan had come in and started to lay the table. Oh God, Hannah! he thought, and it was a cry for help. She came and looked over his shoulder, studying one after another of the likenesses on the paper. Suddenly she bent forward, peering more closely, and he felt her breath on his cheek.

'I know that face,' she said.

He stiffened. 'Which one?'

Her finger touched the paper. 'It's not quite right, though.'

He raised an eyebrow. 'A critical appraisal?'

'No, something's different, I'm not sure what. But I recognize it all right, the eyes and mouth particularly.' She straightened, shaking her head. 'Sorry, I can't place it.'

'If you remember, will you contact me at once? It could be important.'

'OK.' Absent-mindedly she put her hands on his shoulders and began to massage his neck. It was what she'd always done, when he was tired and tense. Now, he suspected she had another motive. 'Finish your drink, then. Supper's ready.'

She moved away, turning off the overhead light and pulling the lamp to the table. Webb watched in silence. He'd let her call the tune; there was a tremendous relief in giving up the fight. Seeming to sense his acceptance, she turned and smiled at him, gesturing for him to sit down.

The kidneys were excellent. She was a good, if messy, cook. In the kitchen, there'd be dirty dishes everywhere, the work surfaces splashed with gravy.

Over coffee, she lit a cigarette, her eyes daring him to comment. Tipping her head back, she blew a chain of smoke rings while he watched the contracting muscles of her throat.

'Have you ever thought of remarrying?' she asked idly.

'No.'

'Why not? You like your creature comforts.'

'I manage very well. I'm a good cook, though I say it myself. Even if,' he added tactfully, 'I've not yet aspired to kidneys Turbigo.'

'Nevertheless there are some things, my love, that you can't do for yourself.'

'They're catered for too.' Forgive me, Hannah.

'I see.' That had surprised her. After a pause, she added, 'You're not the flighty type, Dave. How do you manage, without committing yourself?'

'She doesn't want to be comitted either.'

'Aren't you the lucky one?'

He ignored her sarcasm. 'I think so.'

'Does she know about me?'

'Of course.'

'That I'm here?'

'In Shillingham, yes.'

'You've been with her since I came back?'

He held her gaze. 'That's none of your damn business.'

'What does she do? You can tell me that, at least.'

'She's a schoolmistress.'

Susan's brows lifted. 'Whatever turns you on.' She leant back in her chair. 'And how's the old gang? There were some new faces when I called in. Is the earnest Ken still with you?'

'He is.'

'And Millie, how's she? Still breeding?' Her words were distasteful to him. Had she coarsened, or was it comparison with Hannah which, every now and then, made him wince?

'Since you mention it, she's having another baby, yes.'

'Just the wife for a copper, isn't she? Never complaining, whatever time Ken gets home, and dropping kids at regular intervals. God, what an existence!'

'Which, if you remember, was why you left me.'

She bent forward, grinding her cigarette out on her plate

and twisting the white column of it into the gravy. 'We'd better do the dishes before we start quarrelling.'

In silence they collected the plates and carried them through. He'd been right about the mess. He wiped up the worst of it, while she ran water gushingly into the sink. The tension was building between them. Soon, it would have to explode.

He'd have preferred to wash the dishes himself, since she never got them clean, but to suggest it would only provoke a scene. It had always amazed him that someone so fastidiously hygienic in her work could be so sloppy at home. Stoically he wiped off undetected pieces of onion with the tea-towel. She put the last plate on the draining-board, and pulled out the plug, making no attempt to rinse the sink of soap and food scraps. Then she turned, took the tea-towel out of his hands, and put her arms round his neck.

'I want you, Dave,' she said softly, 'and I think you want me. We both know I didn't only come to cook your supper.'

So they made love, as he'd known they must, and it was as it had always been between them—frenetic, agonizingly intense, but leaving him in the end unsatisfied. And, though their bodies united, there was no meeting of their minds. He knew desire, resentment, guilt, and desire again. The mixture very much as before. Neither of them slept much. They came together several times during the night, and he knew despairingly that she was trying as hard as he to make it right. They'd changed, both of them. They were different people from the last time they'd shared a bed, but they'd grown even farther apart. Despite the clamour of his body, he knew beyond doubt that this occasion was the last. After tonight, they would never again touch each other. The thought brought sadness overridden with relief.

He came fully awake to hear the bath running. What was her assessment of their experiment? He prayed it was the same as his own.

She padded naked into the bedroom and picked up her clothes from the chair. 'Bathroom's free. I'll see to breakfast in a minute.' They weren't quite meeting each other's eyes.

When he reached the kitchen, she said brightly, 'Sorry to rush you, but I'm on duty at nine.' Blearily he looked at his watch. It was still only seven-thirty. 'Toast and coffee do?'

'Fine.'

They ate at the small kitchen table. Beyond the window the Hillcrest gardens cascaded down, one beyond the other, to the foot of the hill, each glowing with autumn reds and golds. And at last Susan said, 'Well? What's the verdict?'

Unwillingly he met her eyes. 'You know, don't you?'

'No, tell me.'

'Susie, we're different people.'

'Not necessarily a bad thing.'

'It wouldn't work.'

'I see. So I've been wasting my time.'

He put a hand over hers, but she angrily shook it off. 'I don't measure up to your lady-love, is that it?'

'It was great. You know that. But we're unconsciously fighting each other all the time, even in bed. We don't seem able to give and take, so we hurt each other. It would be the same as before.'

'Quite the philosopher, aren't you, all of a sudden?' She stood up and collected the carrier bag she'd brought. 'I wasn't asking you to *marry* me,' she added, and he saw she was close to tears. 'I just thought that now and again, for old times' sake—Still, if you don't want me, that's that.'

He stood too, his hands on her shoulders though she struggled briefly to free herself. 'We had six very good years. Can't we just remember those?'

But she wouldn't be mollified. 'It's all right, I get the message. Go back to your toffee-nosed schoolmistress, then, if I'm not good enough for you.'

'I'll drive you to the hospital,' he said quietly.

'No need.'

'I'm going in anyway.'

He followed her out of the flat, pulling the door shut behind him. And it seemed inevitable that, as they reached the first landing, Hannah's door should open and she bent down, hair swinging forward, to take in the milk.

For a frozen moment their eyes locked. Webb forced himself to say, 'Good morning,' as he followed Susan round the next bend of the stairs. He did not hear her reply. Waves of misery penetrated every pore. Above all, it was the sight of her dressing-gown, so dear and familiar, which underlined the risks he had taken. Risks that had been fully realized. And to what end? Self-gratification. That was the bald, unpalatable truth. He'd never believed he and Susan would be reconciled.

Wrapped in despair, he drove into town. 'What'll you do now?' he asked dully, and she answered in his own words of the night before. 'None of your damn business.' A moment later she added brittly, 'Don't lose any sleep. I'm a survivor, too.'

He stopped outside the hospital. She scrambled out of the car and bent briefly back into it, her hand on the door. 'Bye, Dave. Hope you catch your rapist.' The door slammed and she walked, tall and straight and not looking back, up the broad driveway of the hospital.

Slowly he cruised the last few yards to the police station.

CHAPTER 14

The field alongside the Hall was moving with people. At the far end, Jessica could see the revolving circle of a Ferris wheel, hear the excited screams of children. The Michaelmas Fair was in full swing.

'Jessica, my dear!' Leo Sandon was bearing down on them, dressed all in white. 'How delightful to see you! My apologies for not calling again. I've been wrestling with a difficult stanza and I wanted it perfect before presenting it to you.' He smiled vaguely at the Markhams and looked about him. 'Matthew not with you?'

'He's in London,' Jessica said. 'You have met—?'

'Yes, yes. Since you're with friends I shan't detain you, but I'll be in touch.'

Kathy looked after him. 'Is it an act, do you think, or can't he help being like that?'

But Jessica, remembering Leo's outburst at the helicopter, wasn't inclined to treat him lightly. 'He rather frightens me,' she said.

'Really?' Kathy looked surprised. 'I should have thought he was harmless enough. Now what would you like to see first, the flower tent, the stalls or the sideshows?'

Young William interrupted, tugging at Guy's hand. 'Can I have a go at the coconuts, Dad?' Angie, who had arrived with them, had gone with a group of schoolfriends to have her fortune told, a delight Jessica had declined.

'I'd better be a dutiful father,' Guy said. 'We'll meet you for tea in an hour.'

In the flower tent, the schoolmaster and his wife were surveying the children's entries. Donald Bakewell looked as dusty and dispirited as ever, his wife as dogmatic. She must be tiring to live with, Jessica thought. Did Bakewell ever long to break away, to be master in his personal life as in his professional? And could that urge lead to his prowling the village with a Balaclava helmet? She shuddered, disconcerted to find his eyes on her face.

'You're not using crutches,' Mrs Bakewell stated. 'Getting better, are you?'

'Yes, thank you, though my leg aches if I stand too long.'

'Then let's sit for a while,' Kathy said quickly. 'If we stay here long enough, we'll see most of the people we know.'

Jessica was relieved to comply. The sun on the canvas behind her warmed her back, and the air was filled with the scent of flowers. She'd have been more than happy to remain there all afternoon. Kathy leant towards her and said in her ear, 'See that redhead over there? She's a detective.'

Jessica followed her glance. So the police were unobtrusively present. She was more alarmed than reassured. What were they expecting?

The Sandons' arrival interrupted her musing, and they stood chatting for a while.

'You must come to see us again,' Giselle said. 'I regret I have neglected you, and Matthew's research must be almost done. We leave shortly to visit a relative, but we'll be back by the end of the week.' She hesitated. 'I am so sorry your stay here has coincided with all this trouble. It is usually so pleasant and restful.'

Which, Jessica reflected, was what she'd originally dreaded. Now, she would gladly exchange unmitigated boredom for the quivering nerves that alerted her to every shadow.

When, later, they reached the tea tent, Guy had secured a table for them. Jessica caught sight of Lois Winter and waved to her. Everyone seem relaxed and happy, enjoying the social occasion. Was she the only one who studied each man she saw, wondering what lay behind his eyes?

She started as a hand touched her shoulder, and turned to see Della Speight. 'I hear you want some company tonight. I don't mind coming over.'

'Oh, I couldn't put you to all that trouble,' Jessica protested.

'No trouble at all. I'll just pop a nightie and toothbrush in my bag. About eight o'clock suit you?'

'There's no need, really. It's kind of you, but I was only being—'

'Don't give it another thought. Glad to oblige.' And she moved away to join a broad-shouldered man who was waiting for her.

'You could have come to us, if you're nervous,' Kathy said.

'I'm just being stupid.'

What was Matthew doing now? Relaxing in his hotel room, or having tea with his family? Quite suddenly she longed for him with an intensity which was painful. Hey!

she told herself, he'll be back tomorrow! But she wanted him *now*. Wanted to see his large, heavy-lidded eyes, the quirk of his eyebrow, his slow smile; wanted above all to feel his strong arms round her, keeping her safe. Because suddenly, in that crowded, sun-warmed tent, she felt alone, singled out, as though a spotlight were concentrated on her.

She looked quickly about her, seeking the averted gaze, the hurriedly turned head. No one was watching her; why then should she feel she was being studied, auditioned for a part she didn't want to play?

It was six-thirty when, their invitation to supper declined, the Markhams dropped Jessica at Hinckley's Cottage. As she closed the front door, she admitted ironically that Matthew had been right; after a tiring afternoon, she *would* have been happy to relax alone. The prospect of an evening with Della, with her darting eyes and quick speech, was not appealing. Still, Jessica reminded herself, it had been kind of her to offer, and they needn't sit up late.

Not hungry after tea at the Fair, she scrambled some eggs and ate them while watching television. *Phone me, Matthew. I need to hear your voice.* But the instrument beside her remained silent. Silly, she chided herself, they'll be at the party by now. Some guests mightn't even realize the family was split. Would Matthew and that other Angie welcome them as joint hosts? Or was he cast in the role of guest? There was so much she didn't know.

Della arrived at eight. With a perfunctory smile, she walked past Jessica into the room and stopped by the television. 'Oh!' she said, surveying the wildlife programme Jessica'd had one eye on. 'I was watching the other channel.'

'Change it if you like.' How typical of Della's over-familiarity! Yet if she were engrossed in television, at least no conversation would be necessary.

'Ta.' As the programme changed, the room filled with the screech of brakes and rapid gunfire of a pseudo Western.

Two hours, Jessica told herself. Only two hours, then she'd suggest an early night.

But Della, it appeared, was one of those people who, without lowering the volume, liked to talk through television programmes.

'Enjoy yourself at the Fair?' she asked, raising her voice above the sound of breaking glass as one of the villains was thrown out of the saloon.

'Yes, thank you.'

'Did you have your fortune told? She was a real gipsy, you know.' Della laughed and recited. '"*My mother said that I never should Play with the gipsies in the wood.*"'

'No, I didn't bother.' Jessica paused, then added out of politeness, 'Did you?'

'Not me. Carrie's the one for that. Never misses a chance of having her hand read.'

'I didn't see her at the Fair.'

'No, she was working. Matron asked if she wanted the afternoon off, but she said no.'

'And, of course, she's babysitting this evening.'

'For the Plunketts. Do you know them? Young couple just down the road. Couple of kids.'

'I don't think so.'

'You've not missed much. Pretty hair she has, though. Wears it down her back as if she was sixteen.' Her eyes on the cavorting figures on the screen, Della added, 'When's your hubby coming back?'

'Lunch-time tomorrow.'

Della waited as though expecting more information, but Jessica volunteered nothing. Would it look rude if she took out a book? Regretfully, she decided it would. The programme came to an end and Della stood up. 'Mind if I pop upstairs for a minute?'

'The cloakroom's—' Jessica began, but she was already half way up. Jessica gazed stoically at the advertisements. It was going to be a long evening.

'It's *Try Your Luck* now,' Della announced, returning and

seating herself expectantly in her chair. 'Do you watch it? They win fantastic prizes—holidays in America, and caravans and things. The questions are easy, too. I usually know the answers.'

'You should go in for it yourself,' Jessica said, and to her chagrin was taken at face value.

'That's what Carrie says. Why don't you write in, she says, and win us a holiday?'

A large, simpering woman in a short skirt was the first contestant. She selected a number and the compère opened a box and read out the question contained in it. 'What is the most popular name in nursery rhymes?'

'Jack!' answered Della promptly, and, talking over the stumbling contestant, she reeled off quickly, '*Jack-a-Nory, Jack and Jill, House that Jack Built, Jack Spratt, Jack Horner, Jack be Nimble, Handy Spandy Jack-a-Dandy*—'

'Good heavens!' Jessica exclaimed. 'I'd never have got all those.'

'There are more, if you count Jackie. Weird, isn't it, to think how old those rhymes are. Hundreds and hundreds of years, and the words hardly changing. Everyone learns them, and you never forget, even if you've no kids of your own to remind you. You haven't any, have you, but I bet you still know plenty of nursery rhymes.'

'I'm not an authority on them,' Jessica said with forced lightness, 'and anyway they've unpleasant associations at the moment.'

Della smiled and, pulling her handbag towards her, felt inside it. Suddenly, cutting across the television applause, came a voice that turned Jessica cold. '*Curly locks, Curly locks, Wilt thou be mine? Thou shalt not wash dishes, Nor yet feed the swine.*' There was a click and Della withdrew her hand.

Jessica stared at her. '*You?* It was you who phoned me? So it was a hoax, after all.'

'Yes and no,' Della said, and there was a note in her voice which raised the hair on Jessica's scalp. 'I phoned you, but it wasn't a hoax.'

'I don't understand.' She felt bewildered anger. 'What a horrible thing to do. You must have known how I'd feel.'

'Not really, no. You a famous actress and everything. You mightn't be as scared as us country bumpkins.'

Surely there was some way of restoring sanity to the conversation? Unable to find it, Jessica smiled stiffly and fixed her eyes on the screen, where another contestant was now on trial. *Della* had played that tape. But why? It didn't make sense. And why say it wasn't a hoax?

'You see,' Della said, and though she now spoke softly, Jessica could distinguish every word above the mindless studio laughter, 'nursery rhymes turn me on.'

'I can't think why. They're for children.'

'Oh, there's a reason for it. I'll tell you, if you like.'

Keep her talking, Jessica thought. There has to be a simple explanation—she's just trying to scare me. 'All right, tell me.'

'It was my mum, you see.' Della's voice shook slightly. 'She used to have men in, while my dad was on nights. One evening—I'd have been about twelve—my kid sister woke up and started crying. Mum had gone out. I didn't think she was back, so I got up. The cot was in her room, but when I got to the door I heard her voice, all queer and breathless, reciting nursery rhymes—*Bye Baby Bunting* and *Rock-a-bye Baby*.' Della's hand was clenched on her bag and Jessica saw that it was shaking.

'So I put my head round the door to see why she was talking so funny. It was quite light—a full moon—and there she was on the bed with this bloke, rocking the cot with one hand. I stood there a long time, watching and listening to the rhymes, till the kid went back to sleep.'

Jessica moistened her lips. 'It must have been traumatic,' she said. A pulse was beating a rapid tattoo at the base of her throat. She made herself glance at her watch, say lightly, 'Is that the time? I'd forgotten I promised to ring—'

'No,' Della said quietly.

Jessica stared at her.

'No phone-calls.'

'Now look—'

'The phone's off the hook upstairs.'

A burst of applause from the screen assaulted Jessica's ears like a handful of pebbles, sharp and penetrating. She's mad! she thought. I must humour her. But God, she'll be here *all night*! And I can't even move quickly, let alone run away. It was the age-old nightmare, needing to escape and unable to move. But what did she *want*?

She drew a breath. I'm an actress, aren't I? Then *act*, as if my life depended on it. Perhaps it does. 'Why did you do that?' she asked calmly.

'I don't want interruptions.'

'Very well. You have my undivided attention.' She paused. 'You say you were twelve, but your sister was in a cot. I'm surprised you're that much older than Carrie.'

'Ah,' Della said softly, 'but you see, Carrie isn't my sister.'

'Not your sister?' Jessica echoed weakly.

Della smiled. 'I thought you'd have guessed by now. Freda Cowley did.' And as Jessica stared in total bafflement, she repeated softly, 'Carrie's not my sister—she's my wife.'

Webb looked round the crowded public bar of The Packhorse. 'So you've nothing to report on the Fair?'

WDC Pierce shook her head. 'There's a firework display on now, but PC Frost said I needn't stay.'

'We'd no joy either, had we, Ken?' Webb looked at the bar clock. 'Ten past nine. We might as well be making tracks.'

'Excuse me, sir.' The barman stood by their table. 'Chief Inspector Webb, sir? There's a call for you.'

Webb pushed back his chair and followed him to the stone passage leading to the lavatories. A phone was fixed to the wall, its receiver hanging by its flex. He nodded his thanks and the man withdrew.

'Webb.'

'Station Sergeant, Guv. A lady just phoned. Wants you to ring back.'

'What lady, Sergeant?' Hannah? He didn't deserve that.

'Mrs Farrow. Said she'd remembered something and you asked her to phone.'

Susan! 'Did she leave a number?' Webb took it down, said curtly, 'Thank you, Sergeant,' and, fumbling for coins with one hand, dialled rapidly. The phone was lifted at once.

'Susan?'

'Hello, Dave.'

'You've remembered, about that face?'

'Yes, but I'm afraid it won't help. It was just a hairdresser I went to once.'

'But she *is* a hairdresser.'

'That's what was wrong. The one I knew was a man. Funny, though, I could have sworn it was the same face.'

Webb stared at the brick wall in front of him. Some crude graffiti were scribbled there, but he didn't even see them. Beside him, two men came, laughing together, out of the lavatory.

'Dave?'

'Yes, I'm still here. Look, Susan, this could be vital. When and where did you know this man?'

'I didn't *know* him. He did my hair a couple of times, that's all, when we were living in Ashmartin.'

'*Ashmartin?*' Where the unknown woman was raped. 'When was that?'

'Must be three years ago now. Before we moved to Stratford.'

Della Speight a *man?* Webb's scalp was pricking, as though electric needles moved systematically over it. 'Thanks, Susan. If this cracks it, you'll get a bottle of champagne.' He put the phone down and was turning away, his brain already clicking into gear, when it rang again. Impatiently he turned and caught it up.

'Yes?'

'Guv? Fenton again. Thank God I caught you. I've just had Mr Selby on the line from London. In a fair state, at that. He's been trying for over an hour to phone his wife, and can't get through. Keeps getting the engaged tone, but the operator says there's no conversation on the line. Could—'

'I'm on my way.'

Webb dropped the phone and strode back into the bar. The sight of his face was enough to bring Jackson and Sally Pierce to their feet.

'Outside—at the double. I'll tell you as we go. Hinckley Cottage, and pray God we're in time.'

The eye sees what it expects to see. Where had she read that? Believing 'Della' to be a woman, Jessica—and presumably everyone else—had seen him as a woman. Now, knowing otherwise, it took only the slightest adjustment of focus to perceive instantly that he was a man—even though that adjustment made her flesh crawl. There was a bloom of golden hair on cheeks that, perhaps, were not as rounded as a woman's. He'd no need of a wig. The curly hair was unisex, of a length and style suited to both. Now, having acknowledged his charade, he'd let the feminine mannerisms lapse and was lounging in his chair in a frankly male attitude. In blouse and skirt, it reduced his previously convincing performance to the crudest level of drag.

Jessica spoke at last, surprised and gratified to find her voice normal. 'So why the play-acting?'

Speight shrugged. 'I've always cross-dressed occasionally. Then I was in trouble a few years back, so I went over completely and we moved here as sisters.'

'But you must have needed papers—national insurance—'

'My kid sister died when she was three, so I used her name. She was the real Della Speight.'

'Carrie—didn't mind?'

'She was used to it. She lived next door, and we often

dressed up as kids. I was always the girl.' He looked at her
sardonically. 'And in case you're wondering, cross-dressing
doesn't mean I'm either queer or impotent. We've always
lived as man and wife.'

Understanding filtered through. 'Then she wasn't—'

'Raped? No, though it came in handy, accounting for
her condition.'

'And—?' But that question Jessica daren't ask. Nor did
she need to.

'Freda Cowley? Well, like I said, she found out.'

Jessica moistened her lips. 'How?'

'Came back with Carrie one day after the dentist. She
went to the bathroom for aspirin, found my aftershave, and
put two and two together.'

'What happened?' Keep him talking. The longer he
talked, the more time she'd have to plan. The cloakroom
was the nearest room with a lock. But would he allow her
to go alone?

'The next day, Wednesday, was my half-day. She rang
and asked me to come and do her hair. I do go to clients'
houses, so I thought nothing of it. But when I got here, she
came out with it. Thought it was a huge joke, but at the
same time it excited her. Going to bed was her idea.'

He shrugged. 'She might have kept quiet, but I couldn't
risk it. If she talked, the whole new life we'd built up would
be blown. Or she might have put the screws on, which
would be worse. I didn't want to kill her—that's not how I
get my kicks—but I'd no choice.'

'So you made love to her, and then you smothered her?'
In our bed?

'It was quick. She hardly knew a thing.'

'Then you tidied the house to make it ready for tenants.
For us.'

'Right.'

'And sent the keys to the estate agents.'

'Yep. To account for her disappearance.'

'It was very clever of you.'

'That's what I thought. But now you've found out, too.'

Jessica said carefully, 'No, I didn't. You told me.'

'Same difference. I hadn't meant to, though. It was the talk of nursery rhymes that did it.'

'What *did* you intend to do, D—. I don't know your name.'

'Johnnie. Going to rape you, wasn't I, like the others. Wait till you were in bed, then climb up the ivy—make it look an outside job. Quite a feather in my cap, laying Jessica Randal.'

'You could hardly boast about it.'

He ignored her. 'And when it was over, "Della"'d be there to comfort you.' He gave a pleased laugh.

It was a play, she assured herself, not real life at all. Any minute now, the producer would call from the shadows, 'Take it again from—' For how could she be sitting here, in this godforsaken cottage, chatting to a murderer?

'Of course,' she said reasonably, 'it's not like it was with Freda. I'm not interested in blackmail—I've enough money already—and it's not as though I live here. In another couple of weeks, we'll be gone. Your secret doesn't concern me.'

Those masculine/feminine eyes, bright and fringed with stubby lashes, were on her face, assessing her reactions.

'I fancy you,' he said at last. 'Have done since I first saw you.'

'When you did my hair?'

He smiled. 'Long before that. When you first arrived. Carrie told me you'd come, so I went up the road with my binoculars. You were asleep in the garden. I watched you for quite a while, and from then on it was only a question of time. So when she said last night you'd asked her to sleep here and she couldn't, it was the perfect opportunity.'

Jessica stared at him disbelievingly. '*Carrie* suggested you came? Knowing—?'

'No, of course she didn't, and I didn't tell her, neither. This is between you and me.'

'Mrs Markham knows you're here. She was there when you offered to come.'

'She knows *Della*'s here,' he corrected her. 'But what has Della to do with the rapist climbing in the window?'

Jessica held his eyes, seeing the desire there. 'And now?'

'You can take your choice. Rough or smooth, as they say at Wimbledon.'

Panic surged through her. God! she screamed silently. Help me *now*! And her prayer was answered, for Speight straightened suddenly. Then, moving swiftly out of his chair, he switched off the television and stood listening. Jessica, bewildered at the sudden change, stared uncomprehendingly as he turned and raced for the kitchen. She heard the scraping of the bolt and the back door rocking open, before detecting the sounds that had alerted him—voices outside and footsteps on the gravel. A second later, a heavy knock sounded on the door and a voice called urgently, 'Mrs Selby? Webb here. Are you all right?'

For several long seconds, Jessica sat staring at the door, willing her shaking lips to respond. As another knock, louder than the first, shook the house, she managed to call, 'Round the back! He ran out that way!'

With difficulty she pulled herself on to legs that would not support her. The journey across the room was the longest of her life, and when her fumbling fingers opened the door at last, only the red-haired girl from the Fair stood there. She put an arm round Jessica and led her back inside. 'I'll make a pot of tea,' she said.

Webb swore as he rattled the side gate. Locked, damn it. 'Leave it, Ken. There's a field alongside, we'll go that way. He can't have got far.'

'But where would he be making for?' Jackson panted, running at his side.

'Home, perhaps. God knows.' They swung together over the fence and into the dark field, running diagonally across it towards the far end of Hinckley's garden. The ground was rough and uneven. 'Mind your ankles,' Webb warned.

They reached the far end of the field and paused, staring through the darkness ahead.

'What's that building down there?' Jackson asked.

'Looks like a farm. The Davis's, isn't it? Why?'

'I thought—Yes, look, Guv! Someone's moving down there!'

'Come on!' Over another fence and down the grass slope leading to the river which flowed along the foot of the valley. They turned and jogged steadily beside it towards the clump of buildings that made up the farm.

'Jack Frost's son works here,' Jackson volunteered between gasps.

As they reached the farm gates an explosion rang out and they both stopped, looked at each other, then raced with renewed urgency in the direction of the yard. A door of one of the sheds was open, and a smell of cordite reached them. Lying on the floor with a shotgun beside it lay the body of the person known as Della Speight.

'"And the bullets,"' Jackson said grimly, '"were made of lead, lead, lead."'

Behind them came the sound of running footsteps as the occupants of the farm hurried to investigate.

'Best not go inside, sir,' Webb said firmly, pulling the door shut. 'There's nothing that can be done till the doctor gets here. If we may use your phone?'

The saddest part of a case like this, Webb reflected, was the people left behind, the ones who got hurt. In this case, Carrie and Bob Davis the farmer's son, both of whom had loved 'Della'. Carrie at least had known the truth. It was Davis who had the double horror.

'But I was with her this afternoon,' he kept repeating, as they waited in the farm kitchen for the Coroner's Officer. 'At the Fair. She came back with me, to set Ma's hair. Then we—' He turned away, a hand over his eyes. Webb waited patiently.

'It's my fault, what's happened,' Davis said in a choked voice. 'She—he—oh God—watched me clean the gun. I propped it against the wall and locked the door as I always do, but she saw me put the key in the churn. If it hadn't been for that—'

'He'd have found another, perhaps more painful, way,' Webb said. 'He was a confessed murderer, Mr Davis.' That much, Sally'd repeated over the phone. 'He'd have spent the next twenty years in jail, and he couldn't face it. When he knew it was up, he made his choice.'

Davis shook his head as the other aspect of the shock took precedence. 'I can't take it in. *Della!* God, it's foul!'

Webb couldn't contradict him. The old couple, the farmer and his wife, sat at the table with glazed eyes. 'Cruel, that's what it is!' Mrs Davis said, and Webb noted for the first time her expertly waved hair. 'Cruel and filthy, leading our boy on like that.'

'No, Ma, she—he didn't. I never had any encouragement.'

The woman snorted, looked up at Webb. 'Does Carrie know he's dead?'

'Not yet.'

'Poor girl. And her expecting, too.'

Webb motioned Jackson into a corner. 'I'll stay here and wait for the team, Ken. Go back to Hinckley's, collect Mrs Selby and take her wherever she wants to go. She can't spend the night in that cottage. Preferably leave her with friends. Then take Sally with you and find Mrs Speight. Tell her the barest details and leave Sally with her. If I'm tied up too late here, I'll see her in the morning.'

And now it was the morning, and church bells ringing through the village proclaimed it Sunday. Two weeks exactly since the body of Freda Cowley had been found in the ditch.

With a heavy heart, Webb seated himself in the Speights' neat little house.

'I've made coffee,' Carrie said. She was unnaturally calm. Face white as paper, eyes black-circled from lack of sleep, but composed and dignified.

Webb said gently, 'Tell me what happened, Mrs Speight. From the beginning.'

She folded her hands in her lap like an obedient child. 'I've known Johnnie all my life. He always loved dressing up. I used to think he'd be an actor, he was so good at it. He was only a year older than me, and when we were about fifteen we used to go to the pictures as two girls. We thought it was a joke. But we were always sweethearts. There was nothing—funny—about him.'

'Go on.'

'We married when I was twenty and him twenty-one. He'd finished his training and got a job in Ashmartin, so we went to live there. He still dressed in my clothes about the house, but I was used to it by then.'

'You spoke so convincingly of him as your sister.'

She gave a sad little smile. 'When he dressed like that, he became another person. I even *thought* of him as Della.'

Webb nodded slowly. He'd heard wives of other transvestites say that.

'But after a bit I noticed something. Every now and then he'd get restless, like, and go out by himself. He wouldn't take me with him—said he was meeting friends from the salon. After one of these times, there was a report of a rape in the paper. I didn't think anything, but later, I found he'd cut the piece out and hidden it in his drawer.'

She looked up pleadingly. 'He couldn't help it, Mr Webb. It was an illness, to do with the moon. At full moon, he needed to—well. For a long time I daren't tell him I knew, and when I did he went wild. But then he was nearly caught, and we both panicked. We decided to move, and that was when he changed round. He became Della outside and Johnnie at home. And we—we came here.'

'You seemed so established, I thought you'd been here

all your lives.' A major oversight, that. He should have
checked.

She nodded. 'We had services to offer, Johnnie with his
hairdressing and me with my cleaning, so we were accepted
quicker than most. Anyway, I got some Valium and made
him take them every month for the four days the moon was
full. I told people Della had migraines at that time of the
month. And it worked. When Mrs Daly was attacked, I was
sure it wasn't Johnnie. But he'd stopped taking the pills.
Killing Mrs Cowley had got him all worked up again and he
needed the excitement. Like a drug, he said.' She paused.
'I think I knew, then, it was only a matter of time. We
couldn't have gone on much longer.'

'What will you do now?' Webb asked quietly.

'Stay here. It's the only home I have, and my ladies have
been very kind.'

'You'll be all right?'

She nodded. 'I've got the baby to think of now.' Would
she, Jackson wondered, be able to sing it nursery rhymes?
'So if that's all, Chief Inspector?'

'For the moment, yes. Miss Pierce will stay, if you'd like.'

'No, thank you. I'd rather be alone.'

So they left her in the neat little house, alone with her
memories. Though how they could be any comfort to her,
Webb couldn't imagine.

From the Markhams' guest-room window, Jessica watched
the police car leave the village, and some of her tension
eased. It was over, then.

The events of the previous night, ceaselessly replayed in
her mind during a sleepless night, now had about them
the distance and unreality of a dream. The sick horror of
Speight's revelation, the dawning recognition that she was
indeed to be his victim, all now were mercifully blanketed
by disbelief. And although when Matthew arrived she'd
have to go through it again, it would have no personal
relevance.

Yet she knew this respite was temporary. The incidents that had taken place in this village would haunt her for months to come. It would be a long time before she'd remember them with composure, even longer before they were sufficiently absorbed to be incorporated harmlessly in her dramatic repertoire. Only then would the healing be complete.

The sound of an approaching car punctured her abstraction and she rose awkwardly, gripping the sill, in time to see Matthew turn into the drive. Closing her eyes briefly, Jessica drew a breath of pure thankfulness. Then, with a sense of balance restored, she opened the bedroom door.